NAOMI

MYA O'MALLEY

For Alexandra

CHAPTER ONE

Naomi

SHE SENSED IT before she heard the news. She could feel it deep in her bones. All night long she had tossed and turned, unable to find sleep.

Nick.

"No," Naomi wailed into her pillow, pounding her fists.

No. But, of course, she knew it was true. After all, she had a sixth sense about things such as this. *Damn, Nick. Why? How?*

It had been several months since she had taken in his disheveled form, those cowardly eyes scanning her face, pleading for forgiveness from the other side of the depressing, stained, plastic divider at the county jail.

Forgiveness that was difficult to give, although she had been working on it. *Too late, Nick. It's way too late for you now.* Part of Naomi's heart ached for Nick's troubled soul. For the troubled child he had once been.

Another part turned cold as she conjured up his face in her mind. As she had woken from a fitful night's sleep, the image of Nick crying out, lost in the empty dark place where challenged souls lacked peace and closure, was too overwhelming to dismiss as a bad dream.

"Bryce." Naomi spoke his name aloud, even though her fiancé was most likely sound asleep at his house just up the dirt road.

She needed Bryce.

But Naomi knew Bryce would have to wait. Right after her first cup of coffee, she would have to call Officer Marty to confirm the facts of what she already knew to be true.

How had it happened? Possibilities swirled through her mind. Endless scenarios came forth. It could be anything. Nick had been doing time for his part in the cover-up of Maggie Field's death. Prisons could be dangerous, particularly for someone like Nick, a man who struggled to keep his emotions in check and often had difficulty conforming to the rules.

One with a dark, menacing presence.

One with attitude.

Memories of the not so distant past slammed Naomi. Images of Ryan and Maggie. . .

Maggie.

The ghost that had all but consumed her. Maggie had reached out to Naomi, demanding peace. Naomi admitted to herself that she had become obsessed at that time in her life. Preoccupied with putting both Maggie and Ryan to rest. Luckily, Bryce was loyal and patient to the core during the first hectic months of their new relationship.

What would he say now, knowing that a spirit was back? Knowing that this time it wasn't the sweet spirit of a girl named Maggie or a quirky, kindhearted man that needed her help?

This time it was worse, far worse.

This time the spirit was unsettled, tortured—and to make matters even more daunting. . .

He was her ex-boyfriend.

Would Bryce be as understanding about Nick as he had been with Maggie and Ryan? Hopping up out of her bed to make her cup of coffee, Naomi figured she was about to find out.

MOMENTS AFTER SHE hung up the phone with her friend, Officer Miriam Marty, Naomi reached for her coffee mug but then placed it back on the counter with a gentle thud.

Damn, Nick.

Miriam had confirmed Naomi's worst suspicions and provided the bare facts surrounding Nick's death.

He was, indeed, dead. But the strange thing about it was that it appeared to have been intentional on his part. It was too early to say, but Miriam suspected that traces of drugs would be found in his system.

An overdose? Could he have intentionally taken his own life? No, that didn't sound right. Then again, how well did Naomi even know Nick anymore? For that matter, how well had she ever known him? Naomi supposed it was easy enough for an inmate to have the means to obtain drugs. And, let's face it, prison life could be grueling.

No, no. Something didn't feel right about this. Nick's sentence was only to last just a few more weeks, why would he purposely harm himself? As Naomi tried to make sense of the news, she paced the floor. Zelda, her loyal feline companion, weaved in and out of her legs as Naomi stopped and grabbed her coffee mug from the table.

Sharp rapping on the door startled Naomi, causing her to spill her coffee on her blouse. "Shoot!"

Voicing her own displeasure at nearly being stepped on, Zelda screeched as she tore into the living room. Naomi snatched a napkin, wiping at her top as she made her way to the door.

"Are you ready?" Bryce raised an eyebrow as Naomi stepped to the side to allow him through the front door. He leaned over and placed a quick kiss on her forehead.

"Ready?"

"Ah, yes. Remember? We were going to grab a bite and then head over to the trail for a walk?"

Yes. That's right. She and Bryce had plans this morning. With everything going on, she had clearly forgotten.

"I . . . I'm so sorry. Give me a minute to change my shirt. Sit, I'll be right back." She scurried up the stairs to her bedroom to change. This could be a good thing, the time alone with Bryce. His young daughter, Holly, was in school, and she could have Bryce's full attention.

Dressed in a clean shirt, Naomi sprinted down the stairs and grabbed her sneakers. She attempted her best smile as she tied the laces. "Almost ready," Naomi managed.

"What's with you? Why are you out of breath?" Bryce cocked his head as he studied Naomi.

"Just excited to spend the morning with you," she offered a bit too cheerily, glancing up at him as she felt nagging guilt rise in her throat. He wouldn't be happy about the news regarding Nick, and that was putting it mildly. He simply couldn't even begin to understand. He would tell her to leave it alone, not to get caught up in somebody else's problems.

Naomi swallowed hard and gripped Bryce's warm hand as they made their way to his truck. Once inside, Naomi glanced at her fiancé and then gazed down at her lap.

"Bryce?" she whispered.

Concern etched his handsome face. "What is it? What's wrong?" He reached for her hands.

"We need to talk."

CHAPTER TWO

Naomi

WISHING SHE COULD wipe the worry from his face, Naomi gulped. There was no other way to tell him other than to just blurt it out.

"It's Nick." She breathed deeply.

"Nick? I'm sorry, I don't understand." Bryce shook his head, his eyes darting from the road ahead of him to Naomi's face.

Of course he thought Nick was safely locked behind bars.

"Nick is dead."

She turned her head away, biting at her lip. Her heart pounded. This was going to be more difficult than she had anticipated.

"Excuse me? Did you just say that Nick is *dead?*" Bryce released her hand and sat back.

"Ah, yes. I got the news this morning. But I kind of already knew." Her voice drifted as she shared the last part.

There. She said it. Glancing out the window, Naomi silently counted to ten. She got up to three before he cried out.

"Whoa. Back up a minute, Naomi. What are you trying to tell me?" His shaking hands were stilled as he gripped the steering wheel.

Her pulse sped up as she rehearsed the words she wanted to say in her head. "I felt him. Last night. Nick came to me in my dreams." The few seconds it took Bryce to respond seemed like the longest lapse of time she had ever experienced. *Please understand, Bryce.*

"In your *dreams*?" He shook his head, looking out the window. "Wait. Of course." He chuckled harshly.

Naomi fiddled with her fingers, inhaling a deep breath. "Yeah." He knew, he must realize precisely what she was talking about. Bryce and she shared recent history and at times he could read her thoughts and emotions. It was one of the reasons she loved him so much.

"God, Naomi." He pounded the steering wheel with his fists. When he made eye contact, she wanted to reach over and ease his stress.

She spoke quietly, barely a whisper. "I know."

With a huff, Bryce remained silent until he found a place on the side of the road to pull his truck over. "I can't believe I'm going to ask you this, but what does he want from you?" His exhale spoke volumes.

"If I had to guess, he wants closure, just like Maggie and Ryan needed. But closure from *what* exactly, is what I need to find out." Daring to look at Bryce, she blew out a breath when she saw his expression soften.

"And if you don't help him?"

Shaking her head, Naomi spoke up. "You know it doesn't work that way. I wish it did in this case."

"Naomi. I don't want to lose even a piece of you. This whole ghost business took a huge toll on you last time. Hell, it took a toll on *us*." It was true. Finding peace and closure for Maggie and Ryan had come at a price. It was all-consuming. Obsession was more like it.

"You won't, Bryce. I promise." Glancing away, she flinched slightly.

"Don't make promises you can't keep."

"But . . ."

He silenced her by placing a gentle finger across her lips. "Hush, Naomi." Reaching for her shoulders, he pulled her toward him. So close she could smell his fresh, clean scent. So near she could feel the stubble on his cheeks. She breathed in, feeling tears rising.

His kiss silenced her words, banished her negative thoughts. She was home again. In a matter of seconds, he had eased her mind. "We'll get through it. This, this craziness. . ." He chuckled. "I suppose it's one of the things that drew me to you. I'm not going anywhere." And just like that, she was lost in his soft kiss once more.

"THIS WAS JUST what I needed today." It was true. Spending the morning with Bryce, walking by his side along the Hudson River, was the perfect distraction to avoid reality. But eventually she knew she would be alone, imprisoned with her thoughts, and unfortunately, that time was drawing near.

"Please don't drive yourself crazy tonight. Try to get some sleep, you hear?" He pressed his hands down on hers as they stood at her door.

"Want to come in?"

"I can't. I've slacked off enough for one day. I have about two hours, max, before Holly gets off the bus." Of course, Holly would be coming home soon. One of the benefits to marrying Bryce soon would be having the title and all the wonderful perks of being Holly's stepmother. She already felt the strong bond between herself and Holly.

"Sure you can't make it for dinner? Even the president has to eat."

"Don't tempt me, Bryce. I have a deadline with my editor and I probably shouldn't have played hooky this morning." She leaned in to hug Bryce. "Call me after you tuck Holly in for the night?"

"You bet." He tousled the hair on top of her head and gave Naomi a quick kiss before heading back to his truck.

Watching him pull up the short dirt road to his stone house never grew old. In just a few short months, Naomi would be buckling down, tidying up plans for the wedding, and attending to the task of putting her house up for sale. As much as she would miss her home, she knew Bryce's expansive house was the sensible choice to raise Holly and become a family together. Besides, his house held as much charm as her own. Perhaps she would find it held even more appeal.

Thinking back to when Bryce had first appeared at her door that chilly day months ago, she wrapped her arms across her chest and smiled. At the time she had been dating Ryan, but as her friendship with Ryan deepened, their romantic connection became more distant. With Bryce, that spark had always seemed to be present, even from the very start when she pushed her confusing emotions to the side, trying to focus on Ryan. But, of course, she had no idea—and for that matter, neither did Ryan—that Ryan was, in fact, a ghost.

Ryan.

Sometimes it hurt so much to think about him. She missed him terribly, and although she never laid eyes on the spirits of Ryan and his true love Maggie again once she solved the mystery of Maggie's death, she had to admit that she could feel their presence from time to time. From a gentle breeze to the innocent smile of a child, she sensed their warmth from the other side.

Nick. Well, this might prove to be an entirely different otherworldly experience. If Nick had been so volatile in life, what would her ex-boyfriend be like now? The thought horrified her. Would his dark spirit be intensified? Would he intentionally harm her? Foolishly Naomi hoped that maybe last night's episode would be the only time she would sense him.

Naomi laughed bitterly. She was no fool. Nick had unfinished business and as much as she wanted to deny the facts thrown in front of her, she knew he wouldn't rest, if ever, until he sucked her into his disturbed, unsettled world. Hugging herself once more, she fought off the chill that had started to spread throughout her body.

For now, she had work to do. As a contemporary fiction author, Naomi was deep in the middle of a sweet romance. Her editor, Jules, had taken to calling her every few days as a gentle reminder that she was on a strict deadline with her current publishing company. Stated within the terms of her contract, this was the third and final novel she was required to produce. After that, she was able to sign on for another three-book contract or take a small break. In her heart, Naomi had the feeling that her next novel would call out to her, just as her bestseller *Maggie* had done not so long ago.

Maggie, she knew, was her bestselling novel because of how emotionally invested and connected she had been to the story. Obsessing over the tragic events leading to Maggie T. Field's death had served a purpose other than putting two precious souls to rest. *Maggie* had put Naomi in a whole other category by increasing her readers tenfold. Making the New York Times bestseller list in the mystery category had been incredible. Heck, she was still on a high whenever she thought about her success with that book, which was every single day. How could she not when she herself had been so tangled up in the plot?

Naomi allowed her body to relax, leaning against the kitchen wall. This was going to be tough. Tough she could handle, but just how grueling would it be? She held her arms out wide in front of her, knowing that she was being dramatic. But she couldn't care less. "I'm here, Nick! Right here," she cried out to the empty space before her. "Let's do this! I have my life to get on with!"

Nick had never made things easy on her and she figured he wouldn't make this easy, quick, or simple. Her ex-boyfriend was bound to draw this out and torture her existence. Shaking her head slowly, she grabbed Zelda and walked toward her office.

CHAPTER THREE

Naomi

CLICK. DELETE.

Click. Delete.

Click. Delete.

Naomi ran her hands through her tangled brown hair and snickered as she recalled a horror flick where the antagonist, who happened to be a writer, sat for days on end, typing the same sentence over and over again, ever so slowly losing his mind until he went completely mad.

Except this was reality and it wasn't humorous. At least Jules wouldn't think so. *Gee, Jules. I'm sorry, but I can't deliver on my looming deadline because my ex is haunting me, vying for first place as my muse.* No, Jules would hardly find the declaration amusing or credible.

"Let me work, you pain in the butt." Naomi attempted to smooth her hair and pushed her focus on the unfolding love story of two very normal, living and breathing characters. After deleting two more sentences, Naomi pushed her chair back.

"You suck, Nick. You hear that?" Glancing around the room, she didn't notice anything unusual. Nick would make his presence known when he felt like it and until then she would be consumed with worry and anticipation.

There was no sense in trying to work until she cleared her mind. Grabbing for her cell, Naomi called her friend, Amy.

"Are you free for coffee?" she asked. She could brew another pot and share her burdens with one of her closest friends.

"After work I can swing by for a bit. Everything okay?"

"Well, actually no. It's not." Naomi pulled at her hair.

"Oh no—don't tell me you and Bryce are having problems." She could hear the tension in Amy's voice.

"No, it's nothing like that. It's Nick. But listen, it's too much to get into over the phone."

"Nick?" Amy exclaimed. "I can't even begin to imagine. That's one guy who just won't go away, you know?"

Oh, she knew. "I guess you could say that."

With a sigh, Naomi placed her cell phone down and settled in to write. Knowing that she would have the ear of a good friend in a few short hours provided her with the determination she so desperately needed. Her sweet lovebirds continued their love story, page after page.

NAOMI NEARLY CHOKED on her coffee as Amy's expression changed from pleasant to petrified. If she couldn't find some humor in this otherwise bleak situation, she would go stark raving mad, just like that writer from the movie. Naomi explained the Nick situation in detail.

Placing her mug down on the kitchen table, Amy remained silent for a moment before speaking. "You have got to be kidding." She blew out a forceful breath.

Shaking her head, Naomi laughed bitterly. "I wish I was."

"I, I don't even know what to say."

"I don't expect you to say anything, Amy. I mean, what's the appropriate response in a situation like this?"

Nodding her head over and over, Amy just stared at her friend from across the table.

"You're screwed," Amy finally exclaimed.

"Huh. You're right. I'm screwed." Naomi's hands shot up in the air. "Until Nick tells me what he wants, I feel like my life is on hold."

"Listen. There's a chance here that it was just a dream. I mean, I know he's dead, but maybe you just had some weird connection last night and that's it." Amy shrugged her shoulders with a feeble grin.

Pondering the statement, Naomi tightened her grip on her coffee mug. "No, it's not over. I feel it. It's like last time, only different." That was what was scaring the crap out of her. This felt . . . menacing somehow.

"Different how?"

"With Maggie, I felt compelled to help a good person, a pure soul, if you will. But Nick?" She gazed down at the table, shaking her head. "It's as if I don't have a choice. Like I'm being forced to become involved in something I'd rather stay out of."

"Like he's bullying you."

Naomi sat up straight, pushing her hair from her eyes. "Exactly!" It made sense; a bully in life, a bully in the afterlife.

"Wow. I just got a chill through my entire body," Amy stated as she cringed.

"Tell me about it."

"You could stay with me. Or with Bryce, I'm sure."

That wouldn't work. Anywhere she went, Nick's spirit would locate her, she was sure of it. Besides, Naomi was never one to run from a problem.

"I need to face this head-on."

Amy reached for Naomi's hands and gently squeezed. "I know you do."

"I'm worried about Bryce and how all of this might affect him and our relationship. He was so patient with

Maggie and Ryan, but I worry this might just be too much."

"Then don't let it." Amy's eyes met hers. " Don't let Nick consume you. You say he probably wants closure, so find out what that entails and put him to rest for good."

"Yes, yes." Naomi placed her hands on her head and closed her eyes. *Bring it on* was what she wanted to scream from the top of her lungs. Instead, she grabbed hold of her friend's hands, facing her.

"Thank you, Amy. This visit was just what I needed."

"As much as I'd love to stay, I have a date tonight and I have to get ready." Amy winked at Naomi. Ah, dating. Amy was still at it, the internet dates, the blind dates, you name it. Relief flooded over Naomi when she thought of leaving that part of her life behind her. Sure, dating could be fun, but it could also be nerve-wracking and disastrous. Knowing that her future with Bryce was secure made her feel safe.

"Knock him dead, girl." Naomi rose to her feet to see Amy to the door. Once her friend was on her way, Naomi fiddled around in the kitchen, fixing herself a lite dinner of peanut butter and jelly on whole grain bread and a small salad.

Making her way to her office with her food in hand, Naomi prepared to sit and work for another few hours at her desk. Sometimes a distraction or two was just what she needed to clear her head and get back to work. Jules would be pleased with the progress she had made today with her writing. Heck, Naomi might even answer the phone if her editor decided to call her tonight with her gentle nudge.

When her very last word of the evening had been typed and her characters were put to bed for the night, Naomi placed her hands behind her head and stretched her legs. "What is it, girl?" She scooped Zelda into her arms and pressed her face against Zelda's furry body to quiet her down.

The cat wiggled from her grasp, howling fiercely. "Zelda. What on earth has gotten into you?" A prickle of fear coursed through her body as she froze, rooted to the spot. Naomi remembered how tuned into Maggie her cat had been. Sitting as still as she could, barely breathing, Naomi dared to look up.

Words escaped her as she gulped a ragged breath of air. His hair covered one eye as his empty gaze bore directly to her core. Dark eyes, hollow with grief, remained fixed on her. Attempting to rise from her chair, her legs gave way, forcing her back down.

"Nick." Her voice shook as she attempted to swallow back her fear.

And then, just as suddenly as his eerie image had appeared, he was gone.

"Hell," Naomi managed, covering her face with her hands. From around the corner, Zelda peeked her head, watching Naomi.

"Come here, girl. He's gone." But not for long, she knew.

Now she was sure. Now she knew. Nick's spirit was deeply troubled and it was really no surprise given his temperament in life. Dealing with Maggie and Ryan had been child's play compared to what she would inevitably face trying to conquer the darkness of Nick's soul.

Was she ready to take him on?

Did she have a choice?

"SHE WAS SO excited, Naomi. You should have been here. Star of the week, Holly kept yelling all through dinner. Star of the week! Man, she already has the whole thing figured out. From the pictures she'll use on her poster, to the books she's bringing. She'd like us both to come to school that day."

"Yes, that's wonderful," Naomi mumbled into the phone. Her head wasn't into this conversation and as much as she'd love to hear about Holly and her day at school, she couldn't stop Nick from barging into her thoughts.

"Did you hear me? I mean, she was just so cute, I think she's going to burst from excitement over you meeting her teacher and friends, honey."

"Oh, yes. That's great."

"That's it?" Bryce paused for a moment. "What is it, Naomi? Something's wrong."

"It's—it's nothing for you to worry about. I just . . ." Her voice broke off, unable to continue. She was scared. Dammit, she was terrified. This feeling was foreign to her and it frustrated her that Nick, even in death, held the upper hand.

"Whoa. Talk to me. Is it *him?*"

"Yeah."

"Tell me everything, don't leave one thing out."

Naomi gathered her thoughts before speaking. "There's not a lot to tell you. I was writing and then when I finished for the night, I looked up and I saw him standing there, just staring at me."

"Okay, okay." Bryce's brief pause indicated that he was trying to digest her news. "Did he say anything, do anything?"

"No, but . . ."

"But *what?* What else happened?" Bryce's voice rose with increased agitation.

"Calm down, Bryce. He didn't *do* anything. It was more the way he looked at me. Like he was looking through me."

"And then he just disappeared?"

"Yes. But I felt his darkness, Bryce, and I have to tell you—it was terrifying."

"God, Naomi. You have to stay here. I can't let you stay there alone tonight."

25

No, that wouldn't be good. She couldn't expose Nick's disturbing spirit to Holly, or Bryce for that matter.

"I'll be fine."

"Like hell you'll be fine, Naomi. Get your butt over here now before I go over there and drag you here myself." He rarely, if ever, took that tone with her. She enjoyed seeing this side of Bryce, the assertive side that wished to protect her.

She knew that he would see reason when she reminded him about Holly. "There's no way I'm taking any chances when it comes to Holly. I'm not putting her in danger."

She could hear his ragged breathing as he gave in to her. "Damn, Naomi."

"It's okay. I've been through this before. I'm like an old pro at this, a ghost whisperer, if you will." Naomi chuckled softly.

"That's not funny and this time is different." Bryce sighed deeply. "You're right. I feel it, too."

If only he were by her side. Naomi longed to wrap her arms around Bryce, to feel his warm body holding her close, chasing her demons away.

"It's okay," Naomi repeated, this time barely a whisper.

"I wish I could get a sitter so that I could be there with you. I just hate the thought of you alone in that house."

"I know you do, but what are you going to do? Hire a babysitter to spend God knows how many nights with

Holly so that you can be here? This could go on for weeks, months."

Or longer.

"What about Amy or Miriam? I'm sure they would be there in a heartbeat. I'd feel better if you had someone there with you."

He didn't understand. Or maybe he did and was just too fixated on protecting her. "And what? Put *their* lives in danger? I don't know what Nick is capable of, Bryce. Until I figure this out, unfortunately, I'm on my own."

Tension hung thick in the air. For a brief moment, neither spoke. Fear turned to sadness as a tear rolled down her cheek. What would become of her?

What would become of them?

CHAPTER FOUR

Naomi

HE WAS BACK.

Goosebumps prickled her skin. Part of her wished to hide under the covers while the other part wanted to confront Nick head on. She conceded somewhere in the middle. Poking her head out further from the covers, she maintained eye contact with the ghostly form. *Don't show him your fear. He'll feed off of it.*

"Nick." Her voice shook with each breath. This wouldn't do. She cleared her throat; this time her words projected louder, firmer. "Nick. What do you want from me? Why are you here?"

At first he stood, still as a statue. He had to *do* something, *say* something, right? Every moment he stood, his gaze challenging her, she lost momentum. Swallowing hard, she sat up in her bed. "Tell me. Why are you here?

Why are you bothering me?" She shivered as she forced herself to look up at his shadowed form.

The last part earned a ghastly chuckle from deep inside of him. Maybe she was better off with him going back to remaining silent. She needed to be strong, but caution on her part was also required. It had to be a delicate balance.

"Nick. I'm sorry that this happened to you."

She could scarcely make sense of his garbled words, but then he laughed again and repeated himself. "Are you? Are you *really* sorry?" His voice was different than it had been in life. His menacing tone shook her. There was something else—his dominating aura demanded her full attention.

This was not good. She bit down on her lower lip. "Of course I am. I wouldn't wish harm on anyone, you included. Now, tell me . . ."

"Quiet! Quiet!" Nick gripped his head firmly, shutting his eyes tightly. Naomi trembled, backing against her headboard.

"Lies, lies, lies! That's all you women do!" A menacing finger shook with each approaching step. Glancing over her shoulder, she knew he had backed her into a corner, literally. There was no escaping him. She peeked at her cell phone, plugged into its charger on the nightstand. Before she could blink, it floated across the room, smashing into the wall.

Oh, this was not good. Bryce's warm face came to mind. *That's right*, Naomi thought to herself. *Think solid, pure thoughts.* A good man was waiting for her and she'd be damned if Nick came between them. She conjured up her strength from deep within.

"Stop, Nick. Don't!" *Stay strong. You've got this.* "If you want me to help you, you need to rein in that temper of yours." Her breathing came in short, heavy bursts.

His clouded eyes grew darker as he clenched his fists. "Do you hear me?" she pleaded with each advancing step that he took. "Stop, Nick. Stop it!"

"When the hell are you going to learn that nobody tells me what to do?" Nick snarled at her.

She closed her eyes as she feared what he had planned for her. Then she opened them wide as she backed across the other side of the bed, stumbling as she attempted to stand. He appeared there instantly. Sobbing, Naomi wished Bryce was here to help her. Would it even matter? No human could contend with this malevolent force. Nick was faster, stronger, and more volatile than he had been in life. Not a good combination, in her opinion. Not good at all.

His hand, mere inches from her throat, froze in midair. He bit down on his lip, clenching his hands into tighter fists. Seconds ticked by, each one more difficult than the next. She could practically see the wheels turning in his head as she forced her own breathing under control. *Please, Nick.*

"You know, Naomi, for once, I am in complete control. Now I have the power to hurt you, use you, or anything in between." Eerie laughter chilled her. His hand crept back to her neck as harsh memories came crashing back. Thoughts of a time, not too long ago, when Nick was alive, how his hands had crushed down on her neck. Maggie, or rather, Maggie's spirit, had saved her then. Nobody was here to save her now. Nick's hand dropped to his side as Naomi breathed.

"You, you're right. I can't compete with this." Naomi spread her hands toward him. "But you're wrong about something. I don't think you're in control at all. Not of your emotions. You need to calm down and think, tell me why you're here, how I can help."

"You've always done that, you know? The way you speak to me." He tilted his head, mouth agape.

"I, I don't know what you mean."

"Ah, but you do. Don't mess with my head. You speak to me as if I'm a child. Don't do that, Naomi. Don't act as if you're smarter than me, because, honey, you're not." Spittle formed on his lip, dribbling down his chin.

She was trying to calm him, but had only succeeded in pissing him off further. *Let's try this again.*

"I can tell you that I believe you're here for a reason and if you hurt me, then—then you're on your own."

That seemed to give him pause. He turned to walk away, then halted, his black stare pressing on her. " You'd be surprised what I'm truly capable of doing to you. I'm not letting you go. Not this time. " She trembled at the sound of his hollow, threatening tone.

She was then left standing, the only person in the dark room. Naomi dropped to the floor, gasping. Zelda crept stealthily into the room and found her place beside Naomi.

"Oh, thanks, Zelda. Where were you before?" She pulled her pitch-black cat close. "Chicken."

Zelda's soft purr relaxed Naomi, allowing her to slow her racing heart. Naomi rose to her feet, thinking that she wanted nothing more than to hear the sound of Bryce's voice. Legs quivering, she made her way over to the wall on the opposite side of the room, where her cell phone had landed.

"Wonderful." Naomi winced as she picked up her cell. Running her finger over the damaged surface, she sighed. Other than the cracks on the screen, it appeared to be fine. Before she placed her hand over Bryce's name in her contact list, she noticed the time. It was well after midnight. She didn't want to wake him.

"Come on, Zelda." Naomi led the way downstairs. "Let's make the most of this night and get some writing done." Ryan's face came to mind as she recalled that he was always the one she would turn to in times of need, regardless of the late hour, for he never seemed to need much sleep. She missed Ryan so much, and craved his presence.

Naomi headed to her office before changing her mind about her writing. A cup of coffee wasn't necessary. Naomi's nerves were shot; she couldn't sleep if she tried. She figured Nick's recent appearance had been dramatic enough that he wouldn't reappear tonight. One could only hope.

HOW MUCH SHOULD she spill about last night? The question had been forefront on her mind for hours. She wouldn't lie but omitting facts wasn't technically considered lying, was it? In the end she decided she would gauge his mood and then determine just how much she would share.

"Hey, Bryce." Naomi attempted to steady her voice, keep her tone upbeat, perhaps even sunny. It was a plus that they were having this conversation on the phone; otherwise, her shadowed eyes would have given her away.

"Hi, sweetheart. You sound like you had a good night."

"Oh, sure. It was great."

Biting down on her lip, she considered just excluding the topic of Nick entirely.

"What is it, Naomi? What happened last night?"

Damn, he was good. "How did you—?"

"I know you, that's how. You're never that bright and cheerful in the morning, especially considering that you recently saw a ghost."

"Oh, fine. He came back, but then I guess you already figured that out."

"How was it? How did he seem?"

"Well . . . as far as these things go, not good." Pressing down on her lip, she gazed out the window. The peaceful scenery didn't succeed in relaxing her. Even her favorite weeping cherry tree's blooming flowers couldn't do the trick.

Naomi bared every tiny detail. If she was going to be with Bryce, she decided right then and there that she needed to be honest with him, regardless of his feelings.

"Damn, Naomi. We have to do something and quickly. Honestly, I didn't think the guy could behave any worse than he did while he was living."

"I would have to agree with you. He's . . ." Naomi searched for the words. "Broken. Broken and dark."

"And it sounds like you can add dangerous to the list. Do you think he wants revenge? I mean, he obviously blames you for exposing him for his part in Maggie's death."

Of course he would blame her. Maggie's fall from the cliff had been a horrible, tragic accident, a misunderstanding of the worst kind. But Nick had run scared after scuffling with Ryan and ultimately started the sequence of events that led to both Maggie's and Ryan's deaths and the aftermath that had followed.

And Maggie. Poor Maggie. In the heat of the struggle between the two men, they failed to realize how close they were to the edge of the mountain. It was only because of Maggie interfering that Nick survived at all. If she hadn't come between the men, she would still be alive today.

"Yes, I'm sure he feels that if I had left the whole investigation alone, no one would be the wiser." But it wasn't the right thing to do. Bottom line, Nick was involved in the massive cover-up of Maggie's death and had obstructed justice along with his crooked uncle, Officer Frank. And how could she have left Maggie confused and heartbroken for all eternity?

"Then Maggie would still be suffering." Bryce read her mind.

"Yes," Naomi whispered. "Yes, she would. Along with Ryan." Now Ryan and Maggie, soulmates in life, were together after life, finally at peace.

"Come over here, come to my house." Bryce said. She didn't have the time but imagined herself wrapped in his strong arms, relaxing into his embrace.

"I can't. But later, I promise."

"I want to help you but I don't know how." He sighed.

"I wish I could tell you," she admitted. "If I'm going to be truthful here, I feel torn between involving you and just dealing with this on my own."

She wished she could have taken the words back the moment they had escaped her lips. His telltale silence made her wince.

"Oh, I didn't mean that."

"Didn't you?"

She had hurt him. It was the last thing she had intended. "I just meant that you can't help me and I can only cause you and Holly harm. Oh, it's all so confusing," Naomi cried out.

"Listen to me," Bryce stated firmly. "We are a team, we're going to be a family. I can't leave you to fend for yourself here. I will not allow this bastard anywhere close to my daughter, but I'll be damned if I sit back and watch him attack you."

Tears streamed down her face. Her heart ached for him. "I know you'll try, Bryce. I just don't know if it will be enough this time."

Silence on his end signaled that he had ended the call. She would go to him later, give him some space to cool down. Now, she would pay a visit to Miriam.

Officer Miriam Marty had been a witch to deal with during the Maggie investigation. Their personalities had clashed but in the end she was proud to call Miriam one of her best friends and most trusted allies.

After grabbing a cup of coffee that was now a clear necessity, she yawned as she pulled out of the driveway. Bryce hadn't called and he hadn't texted either, but it had only been less than fifteen minutes since their strained conversation had taken place.

The drive to Miriam's condo took about ten minutes. Still, there was no word from Bryce. Naomi's lame attempt to push him from her thoughts obviously hadn't worked. Gathering her purse, Naomi sighed and made her way to Miriam's door.

Miriam never ceased to amaze her. Standing there in her sweats and an old T-shirt, she was just as stunning as ever. The tall blonde officer drew glances wherever she went.

"How is it that you look so amazing, even this early in the morning?" Naomi squinted at her friend.

"Oh, please. Get in here and tell me exactly how you knew about Nick's death. And I want *every* detail." Naomi had briefly discussed the feeling and visions she had received the night Nick had died, but now she went into it deeper.

Once Naomi had finished her story, Miriam's reaction matched Bryce's.

"Back up here. You have to be crazy to get involved with this. But then again, you're you, and well, you seem to attract this kind of thing." Miriam rolled her eyes upward.

Disregarding the comment, Naomi spoke up. "It isn't like I have a choice. If I do nothing, I can guarantee that Nick will haunt me every day of my life. If I help him, at least I have a chance at some peace in the future."

Miriam was quiet for a brief moment. "That makes sense. I suppose you don't have any other option other than to give in to his manipulative plan, whatever that may be. I mean, all preliminary results are pointing to an overdose, whether accidental or purposeful." Miriam tapped her feet over and over. "What type of closure could he be seeking?"

"The hell if I know. Maybe he's just hanging around unsettled and decided to make me miserable right alongside him. You know, get revenge on me for messing around in his, well, mess."

Miriam shook her head, brushing a blonde strand of hair from her eyes. "No, something isn't right about this. I feel it. I asked the pathologist to hurry his autopsy along as soon as I knew that you were aware of his accident. I figured if Nick haunting you wasn't enough to raise a red flag, then nothing was. He wants something from you, it's got to be more than just revenge. What did he say to you again?"

Naomi felt the pressure rising in her throbbing skull.

"Think. It's crucial," Miriam barked.

How could she ever forget? "He said he wasn't letting me go and that he had the power, the upper hand, if you will, this time. He wanted to strangle me, Miriam."

"I'll strangle him if I get my hands on him, don't you worry." She placed her firm hands on Naomi's shoulders. Naomi believed her friend actually would strangle Nick, given the opportunity.

She could have laughed at Miriam's comment if her fear wasn't so strong. What a fool she had been to have ever gotten involved with Nick in the first place. Once upon a time, she had been charmed by him and she should have been smarter.

"Come on, you look like you could use some coffee." Miriam touched the shadows beneath Naomi's eyes.

"You think?" Despite herself, Naomi chuckled heartily.

"See that? That's one of the things I admire about you. You can laugh at yourself and keep a sense of humor, even in a situation like this."

"Yeah, well. I think if I didn't, I'd go crazy. What is it about me that attracts these souls? I mean, I've been thinking. Was I drawn to Maggie because I owned that house or was I destined to buy it in order to set Maggie and Ryan free?"

Fate was something Naomi had been seriously considering since all of this ghost business had begun. What were the chances that both she and Maggie had dated Nick, at different times, of course, but still? Add the fact that she met Ryan while on a blind date with another man. Her existence had destiny written all over it.

Miriam smiled at her. "Honestly, I feel this was all meant to be. And don't ever tell anyone I said that. It's like you're a . . ."

"Ghost whisperer," Naomi filled in, glancing at Miriam.

"Exactly!" Miriam clapped her hands together.

Yes, she'd have to agree with Miriam. Like it or not, she had this talent for attracting ghosts with unresolved issues.

Naomi rolled her eyes upward. "Let's just hope this is the last one in line for my services."

"Now that was actually funny." Miriam smirked as she fiddled with the coffee maker.

"Where's that coffee?" Her energy was waning.

CHAPTER FIVE

Bryce

THE TIMING COULDN'T have been worse. Bryce had some news of his own. News that he wasn't quite sure how to share with Naomi. The more he considered the ramifications of the latest course of events, the more upset he became.

Genna was back. Why? Why now, after all this time? It didn't make sense. What impact would this have on Holly? That was, of course, his first and foremost concern. But in his heart he knew that Genna's presence held the potential to bring stress to his relationship with Naomi. He would simply have to tell her. And soon.

Funny thing was, Bryce had planned on telling Naomi all about Genna's return but Naomi had beat him to the punch with her own news. One fact remained clear—Naomi had a lot more pressing concerns right now than his ex-wife's return, so perhaps he was overthinking the whole matter.

He had come to love Naomi so much in such a short period of time. Blowing out a breath, Bryce clenched his fists. He may not have the power to fight off ghosts, but he would be damned if he let Genna get in the way of his happy life with both Holly and Naomi.

The more he thought about it, he was sure that Genna had most likely been dumped by her latest boyfriend. Or, there was always the possibility that she had simply grown bored of her relationship with the boyfriend. Just like she had grown bored of her marriage and family life. Still, her recent return didn't fit. Genna rarely, if ever, admitted her past mistakes or expressed regret. She had him puzzled for sure.

Memories, the good tainted by the bad, filtered through his mind. Fear was an unwelcome intruder in his life, one he didn't encounter too often. He could admit it to himself that he was afraid for his family, for he knew only too well the havoc that Genna could bring. She was a disaster in the making; everything she touched turned to crap, as far as Bryce was concerned. From her immaturity to her reckless behavior, he knew he would have to hold on tightly to the life he had worked so hard to secure.

On top of the stress of thoughts circling around Genna, Naomi filled his head. Heck, he knew some of his reactions were heightened because of the Genna situation, but how could Naomi think it was okay to attempt to handle Nick on her own? Damn, she was one stubborn woman. Stubborn, yes, but also amazingly selfless, kind, and gentle. No wonder those lost souls gravitated toward her. It didn't shock him in the least.

Picking up his cell phone, Bryce gave in and called Naomi. It had been less than an hour, but he couldn't hold out any longer. Stubborn pride was a useless value, Bryce admitted. He had needed some space and now what he needed was to speak with her.

"Pick up, Naomi. Come on," Bryce muttered to himself, listening to countless rings. So she wasn't picking up. Bryce paced for a moment, thinking that she was going to drive him crazy with worry. They needed to talk, sooner rather than later. He texted her.

Moments after he finished writing the text, his cell rang. At first he almost picked up, thinking it must be Naomi. Genna's name came on the screen and he frowned, turning his cell around. He placed it on the table and wondered what he was going to do about his ex-wife.

CHAPTER SIX

Naomi

GUILT SET IN as Naomi drove to the café for a bagel and some more coffee, and more precisely, a change of atmosphere to clear her head. Knowing that Bryce would be leaving for work within the half hour, she figured she should be at his door, trying to smooth things over. Space was what they both needed more, though. Time to think rationally about this whole ghost business and what it would mean for their relationship.

As she pulled into the familiar parking lot, Naomi felt her heart sink. She and Ryan had come here often together, not that long ago. Ryan's voracious appetite had played a part in enjoying many local restaurants together. In retrospect, Naomi should have figured out that no human could possibly consume that much food and never gain an ounce. Her favorite thing about Ryan had been his passion. Passion for food, history, culture, you name it. Somehow, he still forced himself into her thoughts constantly.

"Oh, Ryan." She dropped her head down and gave in to her fragile feelings. Throughout the entire experience with Maggie and Ryan, through all the good, the bad, the pain and anguish—she wouldn't change having known the two ghosts for anything. Both Maggie and Ryan had brightened her life, changed her for the better. An added bonus to encountering the spirits were the people whom she met through them, particularly Mr. and Mrs. Field. Naomi had grown quite close to Maggie's parents and continued to see them on a regular basis. At least a few times a month they would get together for coffee or lunch. Oh, and Miriam. She would have never met Miriam had it not been for opening up the cold case of Maggie's death.

Only several tables were occupied at the cafe, which was perfect as far as Naomi was concerned. Old habits die hard, she supposed as she chose the table she and Ryan had always occupied. It was tucked away in the back corner, perfect for having a bit of privacy if needed. Back then, they had conversed over coffee and snacks, attempting to piece together the clues of Maggie's mystery. Her heart ached for her old friend and the unique bond they had shared.

Today, Naomi needed a quiet space. After placing her bag down, she glanced around the room and spied the regular waitress who had clearly had a big crush on Ryan. At least now she had finally stopped asking about him. She must have heard the news about Ryan around town. Instead of the exuberant greeting and the questions as to Ryan's whereabouts, Naomi now received an overly polite, if not inquisitive, grin from the young woman.

"Oh, hi there. What will you have today, Naomi?"

Naomi returned her smile with a forced one of her own, and placed her order of coffee and a wheat bagel. It seemed she had become an overnight celebrity in town since news of her role in the cover up had surfaced; that and her bestselling book had cemented her name in the minds of the townspeople.

Within a few minutes, her waitress reappeared with piping hot coffee and her breakfast. More coffee would mean that she might have some difficulty sleeping later, but for now, it tasted divine and that was all that mattered. Her recent coffee addiction was something she should really address, but not now, not with Nick in the picture. It would be high on her list of priorities once she put Nick to rest.

How would she rest tonight anyway, when her thoughts bounced between Bryce, Nick, Ryan, Maggie, and everything in between? Feeling overwhelmed, Naomi concentrated on trying to calm down by practicing deep breathing. She attempted to clear her mind of all of the people in her life and just focus on the moment.

A young man walked up to the counter and paid for his coffee with a smile lingering on his face. What she wouldn't give to be so carefree again. The door swung open and this time a professional-looking man, perhaps a doctor or a lawyer, came into the cafe, scanning the room for a table to sit at. They locked eyes for a brief moment and then Naomi quickly looked away.

He approached, selecting the table right next to hers. Naomi glanced in his direction and was met with a smile. Not wanting to appear rude, she returned his grin and then centered her attention on her coffee. Out of the corner of her eye, she could see him staring at her. Something about him bothered her.

Or nagged at her, more likely. Yes, he had the look of a doctor: professional, tidy, and intelligent. *That's it.* Sitting up straight, she gulped at the sip of coffee she had just swallowed too quickly. Naomi coughed as she tried to clear her throat.

"Excuse me, ma'am?"

She cringed as she looked over at the handsome man. More coughing.

"Are you okay?" He walked over to her, his eyes wide.

"I—yes. I'm fine. Sorry." She cleared her throat, waving her hands, embarrassed by the small scene she had caused. Her face felt warmer by the second.

"Are you sure?" He squinted at her. Damn, he looked so familiar, she could almost place him.

"Yes. It just went down the wrong way." She pointed at her coffee cup and raised her shoulders.

"I'm a doctor, so if anything . . ."

She *knew it.* "Oh no, I'm fine. Don't worry about it." Now she also knew where she was going with her thought process before she had made a fool of herself. If the final autopsy results indicated that Nick had, indeed, died from an overdose, she would try to track down his doctor and see if he or she was aware of any prior recreational drug use.

"Well, I would agree with the fine part."

She cocked her head up at him. "Excuse me?" Was he hitting on her, right here after she had nearly choked up her coffee? She would have been flattered, but there was something about his manner that irked her a bit.

Cockiness. Yes, that was it. She would have never acted upon his advances anyway. Bryce was the only man who would ever hold her heart.

"I think you heard me," he challenged.

Was he for real? Her eyes caught sight of the gold ring on his finger. "And I think you're married. Excuse me." She stood, gathering her coffee, and headed to the counter to settle her bill.

So much for a quiet, uneventful breakfast. Although her back was toward the doctor, she felt his eyes burning into her. Why had she been so aggravated by a flirtatious man? Part of it was his blatantly aggressive behavior, but she felt something else.

Taking one last glance at the man as she walked out of the café, it suddenly came to her. Yes, he was a doctor all right. Now she knew why he looked familiar. He had been Nick's doctor.

The run-in with Nick's doctor was still on her mind. When she and Nick had first started dating, he had come down with the flu and she had taken him to the doctor because he was too sick to drive himself. Nick had insisted she join him in the examining room. Funny, the doctor hadn't made any moves on her then, but she did recall thinking that he had a bit of a complex.

Naomi fiddled with the radio dial, turning the music in her car down. She had too much on her mind and needed to think clearly.

Miriam's call intruded her thoughts. "What do you have?" Naomi answered on the first ring. Naomi's car idled as she remained in her parking spot. The trip to the grocery store would have to wait until she spoke with Miriam.

"Sounds like someone had another coffee this morning."

She brushed off Miriam's comment. "Come on. Any news?'"

"Okay, so like I said before, final autopsy results won't be complete for at least thirty days, maybe more."

"Thirty days!" Naomi yelled into the phone.

"Okay, wow. You need to chill out. Yes, thirty days. But . . ."

"But what, Miriam? But what?" Naomi placed a hand over her thumping chest. She did need to chill out.

"But, the preliminary results are concrete. Looks like our boy overdosed on a lethal combination of prescription drugs. And it looks like it was most likely a suicide."

"No, no, that's not right. It can't be right." A suicide? That wasn't Nick and it was the worst possible scenario for her. How could she avenge a suicide?

"I'm sorry, but let's face it. This doesn't exactly surprise me, not with everything you've shared about him."

"You're wrong. Somebody did this to him, Miriam. He wouldn't take his own life. I'm telling you! Otherwise, what the hell could he possibly want with me?"

Miriam huffed into the phone. "Revenge? Who knows? Wait a minute. His sentence was up in what, two, three weeks?"

"Exactly!"

"Hell. You might be right about this." Miriam sighed heavily into the phone.

Naomi could practically see Miriam pulling at her hair in frustration. "Of course I am. Now what are we going to do about it?"

"*We?* Oh, no. Whatever *you* decide to do with Nick, I'll be here to support you, but I can't go around investigating a case that's not open."

"Then, my friend, we need to make sure it's opened." Her mind was already there. His only known living relative that he had maintained contact with was his uncle Frank. He was on the way bottom of her list of people she ever cared to associate with, but for her plan to work, she would need him.

"Oh, and how do you suppose we do that?"

"Uncle Frank." They spoke his name simultaneously.

"He'll never speak with me. How is that going to work?" Miriam asked, but from her audible sigh, Naomi knew they were thinking the same thing. "No, it's not a good idea. There's got to be another way. We could wait it out a bit–"

"And be tortured indefinitely by Nick's spirit? No, thanks."

"Just be careful, don't go there in person, okay?"

"You bet."

Naomi ended her call and grabbed a pen from the glove compartment. Searching for a piece of paper, she threw her hands up and reached for the next best thing— a napkin. Scribbling down some notes, she would make sense of a timeline after she got everything out of her head and onto the napkin.

"Whew." Naomi wiped her brow, concentrating on her notes. The best course of action would be to start with the doctor. Ugh, just the thought of having to speak with that arrogant man again made her cringe.

Heck, what did any of it matter? So what if he flirted with her? Men flirted with women every day. She would suck it up and make an appointment to see him, regardless. And she would go into his office under the pretense that she was a new patient.

A new text sounded and she realized with a start that it was Bryce. How could he have slipped her mind?

It was happening again. This obsession with the other side.

We need to talk.

Naomi sucked in her breath. She saw that she had missed a call from him. He would be upset with her. He had every right to be. She should have dropped by earlier. She should have called.

Yes. I'm sorry. I meant to call. I lost track of time.

How is it that I miss you already?

Relief washed over her and she laughed, staring at the text.

I know. I'm sorry—for everything.

Dinner tonight? With Holly?

Shoot. With all this Nick nonsense, she hadn't gotten any writing in yet and she planned on trying to secure a doctor's appointment today. Damn, damn.

Sounds great. Can't wait.

Love was about compromise. Compromise wouldn't help her reach her deadline or rid herself of an evil ghost, but it just might make Bryce happy, and that was what love was all about.

Yes, and we do need to talk about something.

Her pulse sped up a bit. *Anything I should be worried about?*

No. No worries.

He was being mysterious. Now she was curious. It would have to wait, though.

CHAPTER SEVEN

Naomi

"ALL RIGHT, ARE you going to tell me what is going on in that beautiful mind of yours?"

She lifted her head to meet his gaze. Her eyes challenged him. "What are you talking about?" She had done her best to keep her bubbling emotions from spilling over throughout dinner. Which, of course, was not an easy task. Heck, she even thought that she had Bryce fooled. She should have known better. It was Bryce, after all. The man should have been a detective instead of a contractor. His instincts with her were always spot on.

"Spare me the act, Naomi. This is precisely what I was talking about earlier." His thumb traced small circles on the palm of her hand. "Don't shut me out. I need you, all of you." His soulful eyes penetrated hers.

"I—I just have a lot on my mind." He was right, she absolutely should be up-front with him, but then why was she hesitating? Why? Because what man in his right mind would go through this again with her? This ghost situation was taxing on her own psyche and worse on her relationships with those around her. In order to get the job done, she knew what was required. Tunnel vision. In other words, Nick would become the entire focus of every breath she took from now until she freed his dark, nasty, bitter soul.

"Don't. Don't do this." Bryce released her hand and stood from the table. He walked toward the kitchen.

"Where are you going?"

"I need a drink." He disappeared around the corner.

Naomi drummed her fingers on the table, each rap growing louder. Just as she was about join him in the kitchen, he approached with a bottle of wine and two glasses.

Bryce placed the bottle on the table with a thud. Glancing at him while he opened the bottle, she knew she had some serious damage control to attend to.

"Bryce, I want to tell you something."

His eyes remained fixed on the red wine he poured into her glass. Placing the glass in front of Naomi, he then poured his own.

"I'm listening."

"I'm afraid I'm going to lose you."

"Afraid? How could you even think you would lose me? Haven't you been paying attention to how crazy I am

53

about you, from the moment we first met? You're thick sometimes, Naomi. Really thick." He raised his eyebrows.

"Okay. I'm sorry and I believe you when you say that nothing can tear us apart." He hadn't seen Nick's spirit, though. The fading image of Nick, his sick laughter, would stay with her forever.

"I mean every word I said. Now, you cannot keep things from me. That's the deal. I can't sit here while you're doing God only knows what and not go sick with worry."

She nodded her head, following along with his train of thought. Okay, she could include him in her plans, keep him informed as to her whereabouts when she went investigating. Her heart tugged with raw emotion as she realized once again how much she missed her partner in crime, Ryan. Last time, it had been so much easier to investigate with him by her side. Her thoughts trailed to Ryan's odd behavior toward the end, which of course was explained away by the fact that he was a ghost and didn't know it. Shaking her head, she knew she wasn't staying on point.

"I understand, Bryce. Please just promise me something."

"What is it?" Bryce came to her side, pulling her up from her chair.

It was her worst fear. Bryce was such a prideful, stubborn man. "Promise me that you won't be placing yourself in danger. It's one thing for me, I have to do this . . ."

"I'm not leaving alone you to scrap it out with an evil spirit. What are you saying here?"

"I'm saying that if something happens to you, Holly will be without her father. I won't have that on my hands."

She watched him clench his jaw and knew he was battling this out in his head. "Damn you," he conceded. "But, hell, will you just get rid of him already?"

Naomi watched as the man she loved struggled with his thoughts and his heart, which was no doubt torn between wanting to keep her safe and protect his daughter at the same time. Tears threatened to spill as she gazed up at him. "I love you. I'll do my best to settle this quickly."

His gaze fell to the floor. There was something else in his eyes. She tuned into his emotions. "What's the matter?"

"Remember earlier when I told you that we needed to talk?"

Of course she did and she was going to ask, but then figured it was just about Nick.

"Yes. What is it, Bryce?" She straightened her back.

"I—wow. I can't believe how nervous I am to tell you this." He gazed at her, not breaking eye contact.

"Okay, now I'm worried. What is it, Bryce?" He was afraid to tell her whatever it was that was on his mind.

"It's Holly's mother."

"Genna?" She scrunched her brows.

"Yes, Genna. She's back. She's here in town."

"I . . . what does that mean?" Naomi's thoughts clouded as she saw the pain in his eyes. For the briefest of moments, she wondered if he was confused about Holly's mother.

Bryce closed his hands around her own, pressing down. "It's nothing for you to worry about. I just thought you should know."

"But, why? Why is she back?" Naomi's pulse sped up, despite trying to appear calm.

"I don't know, not yet. But I do know that I won't let her mess with Holly's head and I won't let her come between us."

What was he talking about? Why did he even feel the need to say that? "I wasn't worried, Bryce."

"To be honest, she's a train wreck but I won't allow her to bring her drama into our lives. I promise you that. Naomi, I love you more than I could have ever thought possible. You and I, we're stuck with one another." He kissed her cheek lightly.

A train wreck? That didn't sound good, but Naomi trusted Bryce when he said he would handle the situation. Neither she nor Bryce needed additional stress at this point, not with everything else going on. She would be supportive.

Naomi forced a smile. "Well, I'm glad to hear that. And Bryce? Please don't even worry about me. I love you and I won't let anything or anyone come between us. You're stuck with me, too." She winked, earning a chuckle from him. She did wonder how Holly was going to be affected by the return of her mother and worried for her.

Bryce's warm eyes crinkled as he gazed at her. He leaned forward, pressing his mouth on hers. Her emotions were high, as were his. Her pulse quickened at his touch as the kiss grew deeper. Bryce broke their kiss, his gaze penetrating through her.

"Bryce," she breathed.

"Come with me." He guided her toward his office down the hall and locked the door behind them. He pulled her down on the floor and soon she forgot about Genna, Nick, and all the ghosts from her past.

STREAMING SUNLIGHT FILTERED across the room, waking her gently. Incredibly enough, Nick had not graced Naomi with his presence during the night. Nor had she been plagued by nightmares. Who cared why she was given a reprieve, she would take it. After the night she had shared with Bryce, she felt positive about their future. All thoughts of Genna were long gone. The time alone with Bryce was exactly what they had both needed.

"You know what, Nick?" she called out, feeling refreshed. "I'm not afraid of you. We'll deal with this unfortunate situation and then you'll leave me to get on with my life."

She was met with silence. Hm. Where was he? And for that matter, where did ghosts go when they weren't lurking around?

"Well, fine. I'm pretty sure you can hear me. I have a book to write, and an appointment to make." Shaking her head slightly, Naomi chuckled as she considered what others would think of her walking around talking to herself.

It was too early to call the doctor's office, but never too early for a cup of coffee. Coffee first, then she needed to make up for the time she had lost with her writing yesterday.

Words flowed seamlessly as Naomi made the most of her upbeat mood. After practically begging for an appointment with Nick's doctor, which she had no luck securing on such short notice, she had received a follow-up call stating there was a last minute cancellation for a late afternoon appointment. She would need to figure out the best questions to ask. She couldn't just come right out and ask what he knew about Nick's supposed drug problem.

Seconds had slipped to minutes and now Naomi realized she had completely lost track of time as at least a half hour had passed. Nick had invaded her thoughts and interrupted her writing once more. Gone was her carefree mood. *Nick, tell me what you need me to do.*

It wasn't that easy and she knew it. Even Maggie's kind soul had such difficulty conveying her thoughts to Naomi. Maggie had spoken in riddles and then she had eventually pieced together the clues and solved the puzzle of her death. Nick was being a tyrant. He projected his words more forcefully and in a more direct way. Then why the hell couldn't he just come out and speak to her, tell her what happened?

A chill prickled Naomi's scalp as she heard a strange noise. She turned around, instantly locating her cat across the room. It was coming from upstairs and it sure as hell wasn't Zelda making that racket.

With each approaching step Naomi took up the stairs, the sounds grew louder. One of the voices she detected sounded an awful lot like a woman. No, not just any woman, but Maggie. Or rather, a distorted version of Maggie.

Afraid of what she would find when she walked into her bedroom, Naomi tried to steady her thumping heart. She would need to confront Nick and his demons head-on.

He stood holding his head, wailing. She heard Maggie screaming, she heard Ryan, and yes, Nick. What was she witnessing? The only person in the room other than her was Nick. But how was he doing this?

He faced her, eyes black and soulless. Sucking in her breath, she walked backward toward the door.

"Oh no, you don't," Nick's words boomed. "You get to join me in the fun." His sick eyes gleamed as his hand reached out for her. Sucked back into the center of the bedroom, she fell to the ground with the force of Nick's spirit pushing her. Now it was just her and Nick, the other voices a play on his thoughts—a trick of the mind.

"No, no . . ." she wailed, crying out for someone to help her.

Beside her, Nick sat on the floor. She could feel him there, but was afraid to look. Heavy arms pulled her into his dark embrace.

And then she saw what plagued his troubled mind. She saw, from his point of view, Maggie and Ryan falling to their deaths from that high cliff, his hand reaching out. He was too late. She felt the depth of his fear, his grief. The images he had shared with Naomi sucked her down into her own place of bleak despair.

Darkness dissipated and her ragged breathing slowed. He had been gone for minutes, she knew that, but she wasn't ready to open her eyes. He wouldn't make this easy for her. He would make her suffer, just as he had. Nick would make Naomi feel every ounce of the pain he had experienced, even more if he could muster it.

He could make it so much easier on both of them. She knew he could.

But he wouldn't.

It was to be a game of cat and mouse. Just how long would he make her suffer?

CHAPTER EIGHT

Naomi

"NAOMI?" A YOUNG nurse called out from the doorway. "Naomi?"

"Yes." Naomi stood and then followed the woman down the long hallway and into one of the examining rooms.

"Right here, room six."

"Thank you." Naomi sat on the examining table, making small talk as the nurse asked her some questions and took her vitals.

"Are you nervous today?"

"Um, a bit, I suppose."

The nurse asked Naomi to try to relax and then took her blood pressure again. Ripping the Velcro apart, the nurse studied Naomi.

"Is your blood pressure normally high?"

This was no surprise, considering all she had been through and the purpose of her visit.

"Normally, no. Lately, yes." And, of course, her two cups of morning coffee couldn't have helped.

Her comment drew a stare from the nurse. "Well, then you can discuss it with the doctor. He should be right in."

She was pretty sure her blood pressure had skyrocketed higher upon hearing that the doctor would soon be joining her.

As she fidgeted on the examining table, she tightened up her plan of action. What was with these doctors? Each and every time she had an appointment, she was left waiting in the room for at least fifteen minutes, sometimes more.

Naomi hopped off the table and grabbed her cell. She checked the time and realized she had been sitting in this room for close to twenty-five minutes. She stretched her back from side to side, grumbling to herself as the doctor walked into the room.

"Hi there, Naomi." His bright smile froze as she saw slow recognition register on his face. He remembered. At first, he cleared his throat, then looked away. A penetrating stare came next. Finally, the doctor smiled again, this time not quite so wide.

"Hi, Doctor Bender." Naomi jumped back onto the table and swung her legs. She gave him her sweetest smile. Oh, this might end up being entertaining.

The doctor gathered himself and nodded at Naomi. "I apologize for any rudeness I might have displayed before, you know . . ."

She cocked her head, not letting him off the hook. Maintaining eye contact, Naomi raised her brows, waiting for him to continue.

"I, uh. I don't make it a habit out of trying to pick women up at coffee shops," he stated. "Just thought you should know."

Naomi nodded her head. "Great. Good to know."

Dr. Bender scratched at his head. "And I trust that we can keep this between us."

"Of course." There was no point in riling up the good doctor. She would play nice.

"So, what you brings you in? I hear you're looking for a new doctor."

"Yes. I'm kind of shopping around, so to speak. But I heard wonderful things about you, so here I am." Naomi lifted her hands wide in the air, plastering on a grin.

"Well, how kind of you to say that, especially after, well, you know."

She thought he would drop the whole subject, but apparently he wasn't letting it go. "Anyway. Your receptionist said that you're booked a month or so for physicals."

"How long has it been since your last?"

"Oh, I'm overdue so I'll make sure to book an appointment on my way out."

"Glad to hear you're staying." His eyes lingered on her for a moment too long.

She fidgeted, moving her bottom on the table. "That's yet to be determined, Dr. Bender. I came here today to discuss my chronic back pain." She set her plan into action: let's just see how quickly the doctor gives out heavy-duty pain meds.

"Sorry to hear that you're in pain. What's the cause of the pain?"

"I fell a while back. One second I was taking the trash down the stairs, the next second I was lying at the bottom of the stairs surrounded by garbage." That seemed a pretty credible story. A little bit too much information, but plausible just the same.

"Oh, what a mess. No pun intended, of course." Dr. Bender chuckled.

Naomi shook her head. What a cornball. "So here I am." She raised her hands and looked into the doctor's eyes. "What can you do for me?"

"Let's have a look. Just lift your top a bit?"

Naomi eyed him warily but did as he instructed. With only her lower back exposed, he felt around, pressing here and there. "Is this painful?"

"Only a bit when you touch it. It mostly hurts when I'm sitting or standing too long. Some days I can barely get out of bed."

"How long have you had this pain?"

"I don't know, say, at least six months."

"Six months? Have you seen a doctor? Besides me, that is?"

"Doctors, chiropractors, you name it. Nothing helps. I even had physical therapy."

"Well, it sounds like we should have an image of the area, then. Let's go ahead and order an MRI and then we'll see what it is we're dealing with."

"Oh, please don't waste my time on another MRI. The last doctor ordered one and it showed a herniated disc. The only thing that helps is painkillers."

He raised a brow at her. "How about starting with ibuprofen? You can take up to six hundred milligrams every four to six hours."

"Ibuprofen? That's child's play, Dr. Bender." She rolled her eyes dramatically. "I'm way past ibuprofen. My last doctor prescribed Percocet."

Dr. Bender shook his head. "Whoa, Naomi. Slow down here. Most slipped discs that are going to heal naturally will do so within a month, perhaps six weeks. If you're still suffering after six months and nothing else has worked, you may end up needing surgery."

"Surgery? No way." Naomi played the part well, shaking her head. She should have done better research about back pain. So far, this wasn't proving to be a slam-dunk, but she was pretty confident if she persevered with this herniated disc act, the doctor would soon give in. She was aware of the high rate of dependence from taking Percocet for a long period of time. Opioids were highly addictive. Perhaps Nick had started off taking just a few pills here and there and then found himself in trouble. It wasn't a stretch to see how such a drug could be obtained in the county prison.

"Why not? Excuse me, Naomi, but what did you say the name of your previous doctor was? I didn't see any information about past medical records in your file."

Shoot. She would have to play the card she was hoping to avoid. "I didn't say, Dr. Bender. However, I'm pretty sure if word got around about how overtly flirtatious you were with me back at the coffee shop, your wife might not understand." She glanced up, batting her eyelashes at him.

He leaned in, so close that she could smell the coffee on his breath. "Are you threatening me? Blackmailing me because I *flirted* with you? That's hardly grounds for me giving you drugs."

"Oh, no. I think you misunderstood. You see, I believe we got off on the wrong foot and I think we should start over. I want painkillers. Maybe Percocet? Vicodin?" She smiled sweetly, waiting him out.

"You're a brazen one. I bet you don't even have a problem with your back. Am I right?" He drew closer, his eyes narrowing in on her.

Shrugging her shoulders, she laughed. "Does it really matter?"

"Of course it matters. I am not giving you anything but advice to grab some ibuprofen from your pharmacy. Say what you will, I'm not worried."

As Naomi considered her next move, the doctor studied her for a moment and then walked over to the small table where her chart lay. Naomi watched as he shuffled through the papers. His expression changed to disbelief.

"Wait—I knew you looked familiar. I've seen your picture in the paper. You're an author. You wrote that book that exposed . . ."

"Nick?"

"Yes. Nick." Was it her imagination or did the doctor turn a paler shade at the mention of his name?

"That's me. Now I don't have all day. Are you going to give me what I want?" She tapped her fingers on her thighs.

"Fine." He sat down and quickly typed on his keyboard. "I didn't figure you as an addict, but hey, why should anything surprise me anymore? I sent some painkillers with several refills over to your pharmacy. Do me a favor?"

Rising from the table, she stood up straight, meeting his gaze directly. "Yes?"

"Don't come back. You're not welcome here."

"And if I need more?" She challenged him, continuing the part.

"Dammit. Get out of here. Just get out of here." He looked at the floor as Naomi walked toward the door.

"Let me ask you something else while I'm here. Since we were just on the topic of Nick, how easily did you give up painkillers to him? Was it as easy as it was for me?"

Dr. Bender stepped in to meet Naomi. "I don't know what game you're playing here, but I would advise you to mind your business."

"And if I don't?" She crossed her arms over her chest.

"Get the hell out of here." His breath hit her face. Naomi realized she didn't like the look in his icy eyes. He was either extremely pissed or scared. She figured it was most likely a combination. She also knew her time was up with Dr. Bender.

CHAPTER NINE

Naomi

TRUE TO HER word, Naomi kept Bryce informed about her recent visit with Dr. Bender. She had started to tell him about how her plan unfolded when he interrupted her and told her that he would be over in a few minutes.

Bryce wasn't happy. That was the problem with telling him every freaking detail of her plan. Torn again between sharing openly and being cautious with what she disclosed, Naomi's thoughts were interrupted by the harsh knock on her door.

"Hi, honey." Naomi reached up and kissed Bryce. He brushed past her, barely allowing her lips to graze his cheek.

"Are you crazy? Making an appointment with Dr. Bender to try to what, catch him in something? What is going on in that head of yours? Do you know that Dr. Bender is highly respected in this town?"

"So what? Do *you* know that he's a creep, scratch that, a *married* creep that hit on me yesterday at the café?" And she wanted to add that in addition to the flirting, he handed over dangerous, addictive painkillers, way too easily.

"What? I don't even know what you're talking about. What did you expect to accomplish by going over to his office?"

"If you just calm yourself and open your mind to this, then I will tell you." She pointed a finger at the table. "Now sit. I'm going to put on a pot of coffee and then we will talk about this calmly." She had to tell him everything.

"I think you've had too much coffee as it is," Bryce huffed as he sat down.

As Naomi prepared the coffee, she remained silent. She could hear Bryce's heavy sighs and figured he needed a minute or so to relax.

Setting the mugs down on the table, Naomi took a deep breath before she continued. "As I was saying . . ."

Bryce's hands were clenched into tight fists. She reached over and loosened his grip, holding on to his hands gently.

"Miriam and I have reason to suspect that there is foul play involved here."

"Of course there is," Bryce muttered, his head down.

She raised her brows at him and then continued. "Preliminary reports show that Nick overdosed from what we believe may have been a combination of Percocet and other painkillers. Why would he kill himself when he only had a few weeks until he was due to be released?"

"Maybe it was accidental."

She had considered that. Even so, if the doctor had given Nick the painkillers to begin with, she could imagine that Nick may blame Dr. Bender for getting him hooked. In that case, what was she supposed to do? She glanced at Bryce, but he had averted his eyes to the table.

"It very well could have been. Regardless, something stinks here. I made the appointment with Dr. Bender under the pretense of trying to obtain drugs."

Bryce spun his head to face her. "Have you lost your mind, Naomi?"

"No, on the contrary." She smiled. "I thought I was quite clever." She was actually pleased with her performance this afternoon. Well, maybe she shouldn't have outright accused him of giving Nick the painkillers, but that part kind of just slipped out.

"Please, please, please tell me you didn't do anything stupid."

His comment irked her. "Excuse me?"

"Go on."

"Fine. At first he was playing it straight, even when I told him that his wife wouldn't be pleased to hear about him hitting on me, but guess what? When he recognized me from the news and made the connection to Nick, he couldn't have written the prescription faster if he had a gun to his head."

"Oh my God. You *have* lost your mind. You have *completely* lost your mind." Bryce raked his hands through his thick hair, a habit she was growing accustomed to seeing whenever he became frustrated.

Gazing up at her, Bryce spoke again. "What do you think you are, a detective or something? You're *not*, Naomi. You shouldn't be running around trying to solve crimes like this. For heaven's sake, you're an *author*, not a cop. Do you realize you just tried to blackmail one of this town's favorite residents?"

Oh please, he was being dramatic here.

Crossing her arms over her chest, Naomi sulked. Bryce was losing his cool much earlier than she would have anticipated. She supposed the whole Maggie and Ryan thing hadn't helped. He had witnessed her in danger before and now that they were engaged to be married, well, she supposed it was all coming from a place of concern.

"Please try to understand. This Dr. Bender is *far* from an upstanding guy. Think what you will, but he was downright pompous when he made a move on me and he was pretty quick to give me whatever drug I wanted."

"Naomi. You threatened to tell his wife and I'm sure he feels awful about Nick. I can't believe you would do this. And to what end? What have you gained by getting addictive drugs from him? I don't get it."

"First of all, I'm not going to fill the prescription," she huffed, rolling her eyes upward.

"Not the point." His gaze bore into her.

She stood, walking back and forth as Zelda weaved around her feet. "I wanted to see how easily someone, like Nick in this case, could get drugs from the doctor."

"And? So what? Maybe Nick really did suffer from pain. Let's even go as far to say that he became addicted and Dr. Bender continued to supply him with drugs for his pain. What now? What does any of this prove?"

"It's a start. If Nick became addicted, he would naturally increase his dosage as his body adjusted to the medication. He would need more to feed his habit. If that was the case, Dr. Bender could be proven negligent."

"Who's to say he even got them from the doctor in the first place? And for argument's sake, if he did obtain the drugs from Dr. Bender initially, the doctor certainly didn't continue to supply the drugs from behind the walls of the prison."

Damn. He did have a point. It would be hard to bring down a doctor for creating the beginning of an addiction. Surely whomever supplied the drugs in the prison would be to blame.

"Okay. You have a point," she conceded. "But, I need to see the big picture here and this was a good place to start." She omitted from the conversation her last words with Dr. Bender, the harsh accusation.

73

Bryce remained silent, no doubt considering her words. "I can understand that, Naomi, I guess, but *blackmailing* him for *flirting?*"

"Okay, so maybe I pushed the envelope a bit, but he didn't care about that anyway." She glanced away.

"A *bit?* You think?"

She saw him softening. His mouth turned up slightly and his eyes met hers.

"Just a little bit." Naomi pressed her fingers together.

"You're crazy, you know?" He stood and reached for her.

"But you love me anyway." She snuggled into his shoulder.

"You drive me nuts with worry, Naomi. But, yes, I love you."

He lifted her chin and she melted her mouth against his, breathing in his cologne. He bit down softly on her lower lip, his tongue touching hers.

"Bryce." She broke free and kissed up and down his neck. He shivered, then scooped her in his arms, leading her into the living room. He placed her softly on the couch.

Lost in the moment, Naomi kissed him as he pressed against her, their kisses growing more urgent with each breath. At first, she disregarded the noise. It was probably Zelda, messing around.

The sound grew louder, more insistent, demanding her attention. It was howling, a scream, and it wasn't a sound that could possibly come from a cat. No, only one thing could be capable of creating such a noise.

"Bryce!" She sat up, covering his head with no time to spare. A vase from her table blasted right past Bryce's ear—millimeters away from making contact. Nick's glinting eyes bore through hers, his grin maniacal.

"Naomi!" Bryce covered her with his own body, shielding her from a stack of books that whizzed past them.

"No! He won't hurt me. He needs me! Bryce, get out of here!" She was the one who should be protecting Bryce. She tried to squirm out from under him, but Bryce was too strong for her. Didn't he see? Bryce was the one in real danger here.

"Go away, Nick! Go away!" she screeched, desperate for him to stop this madness. "You hurt one hair on his head and you're on your own! You hear me? Do you hear me?" Hysteria rose in her voice. It took a moment, but then all was instantly silent. Eerily quiet. Even Zelda didn't dare make a sound, but her eyes were fixed on Naomi.

Minutes passed before Naomi even realized she and Bryce were sitting, side by side, neither talking. When she dared to look at him, she saw the muddled emotions playing on his face.

"Bryce . . ." She reached for him.

He turned to face her. "Naomi." He stood slowly, legs quaking. "What you're dealing with here—it's nothing like before."

"I, I told you that."

"Come home with me. Right now. Come with me." He took her hands in his, squeezing them.

Her eyes dropped to their entwined hands. "I can't. I won't." He knew she would never put him and his daughter in danger. He knew it. But accepting it was another matter.

"He'll find me. Wherever I go, he'll find me. But remember that he also needs me. It's a fine line he's walking and it's my job to keep him on his toes."

"I'm not so sure he *needs* you for anything, Naomi. Have you considered that maybe he just wants to bring you down, make you suffer as much as he has?"

Miriam had pretty much suggested the same thing. If Nick was, indeed, solely seeking revenge, then it was hopeless. She wouldn't allow herself to believe that scenario.

She could see the frustration rising from him, from the grimace on his face to the way his shoulders slouched. "I hope you know what you're doing, sweetheart."

She hoped so too.

CHAPTER TEN

Bryce

HOW COULD HE have expected that Genna would just go away and leave him and Holly alone? Dammit, he should have demanded in their divorce agreement that he received full physical custody of their daughter. At the time, Genna had taken off with her new boyfriend and willingly signed their divorce agreement. His lawyer had advised fighting for custody but Bryce was worried that with things going so smoothly, he just might piss Genna off enough that she would try to take Holly away from him. He was in such an emotionally vulnerable place back then and he knew how Genna's brain worked. If she got wind that he was worried about custody, she might have stirred up a whole lot of drama. Honestly, Bryce didn't predict her return, but with hindsight, he should have.

What would happen now if she sought out anything other than visitation? With her past alcohol abuse and track record of men, not to mention the fact that Genna had left her own daughter for over a year, he doubted that any judge in his or her right mind would grant her custody. But you never really knew, did you? Stranger things have happened.

It didn't do any good to worry about what he couldn't control right now. Easier said than done, he figured, as he spied Holly coming around the corner, a huge grin on her angelic face.

"Daddy!" Holly gushed as she ran over toward him.

"Hi, sweetie." Leaning over, he kissed the top of his daughter's head, then tousled her long, brown hair.

"So I was doing some thinking," Holly stated dramatically, her hand rising to rest on her chin. This was the new phrase she loved to spout.

Uh-oh. The statement was usually followed by an outlandish idea. "Yes, honey. What were you thinking about?"

"Well, I know that Nomi is going to be your wife and everything," Holly began. Funny, she was so precocious for a first grader, but she still mispronounced Naomi's name in the most adorable way.

"Go on." Oh, this was going to be interesting. He waited out his daughter's dramatic pause.

"I think that she should share my bedroom with me, since she's going to be my mommy."

Just as he figured, Holly's mind was always working overtime. With a deep sigh, Bryce considered his next words carefully.

"Yes, Naomi is going to be like a mom to you, honey. But did you know that moms and dads share their bedrooms?" Most did, that is. He knew several of his friends actually slept in separate bedrooms although they were still married.

Crossing her arms across her chest with a huff, Holly then stomped her feet. "That's selfish, Daddy!"

"Now, Holly. I would like you to speak kindly to me." It wasn't often that his daughter was snippy with him, but it was essential that he remain firm, albeit calm, with Holly when she acted out. He also needed to explain that although Naomi would be like a mom to her, she did, indeed, have a mother. And one who very well might be coming to visit soon. The latter part he would keep to himself for now.

"Sorry." Holly's lower lip jutted out as she rolled her eyes upward to the ceiling. A flash of what Holly might look like as a teenager flashed before him. *I can't even begin to imagine.*

"You know, there's something I want to talk about." Watching her chin turn to the side, he saw her attitude shift. That was one of the wonderful things about Holly. She didn't hold grudges very often.

"You know that Naomi loves you very much." Bryce glanced at Holly, who nodded along as he spoke. "You do have a mother, too." It was heartbreaking to see the stress come over her tiny face. It had to be awful to see all the other kids at school who had both a mommy and a daddy. He had tried so hard over the past year or so to be both mother and father to his daughter. Some things you just couldn't change, though. He knew that Genna's disappearance would ultimately leave some type of scar.

"Where is she?"

He detected the smallest quiver of her chin as he continued. "Well, we've spoken about this before." He was stalling and Holly was clever enough to see his hesitation.

"I don't like her. No sir, not one little bit. Naomi is my mom." She placed her hands on her hips and huffed as she turned and headed up the stairs.

"Holly!" He called after her, wishing he could take the pain from her and swallow it up himself. Unfortunately, life didn't work that way. She was growing up and he couldn't protect her from everything, as much as he attempted to.

Bryce's reaction was to punch the wall, but he stopped himself just short of doing so and counted to ten silently. It had been a strategy he had used often, back when Genna had first left. Knowing what he needed to do, he grabbed the phone and called Naomi. After explaining the situation to Naomi, he felt better. Naomi promised to come by later before Holly went to bed and speak with her. For now, he would head upstairs and gently comfort Holly. There was no need to say too much regarding Genna; for all he knew she might just pack up and leave without even requesting to see Holly. Bryce could only hope.

Creaking sounded from the hallway before him as Bryce made his way up the old stairs. He spun his head in the direction of the sound but nothing was there. It was probably just the aging home working out its kinks.

Holly's door was ajar. Peeking in the room, he watched Holly playing with her dolls. From the sound of it, she was working out her troubles through play. Wasn't play therapy exactly how kids her age figured out their worries?

"Sweetheart?" He pushed the door open and walked into the room. Holly's gaze met him and he swallowed. He fought back his own tears as he watched Holly wipe at her eyes.

Sometimes words weren't needed. He wrapped his arms around his girl, taking in the fresh, clean scent of her shampoo. "I love you, sweetie. You are very loved. Please don't ever forget that. Your mom, she loves you too, but she has some things she's working out and she needs to get herself together."

"Is she sick?" Holly's voice cracked.

"In a way. But it's never been about you. Never. How could anybody not love you?"

That earned a smile from her. "Am I still your most favorite person in the whole wide world?" Her hopeful face nearly broke him.

"Of course you are, silly. You don't even need to ask."

Bryce hid his tears as he pressed his head down to meet Holly's.

CHAPTER ELEVEN

Naomi

WHAT NEXT? NAOMI considered her options but the problem lay in the fact that there didn't seem to be many possibilities. Where should she turn? She had placed a call to Uncle Frank and wasn't shocked that he hadn't called her back. Miriam had already warned Naomi about her former partner's temper.

Miriam was right, she should give Uncle Frank some time and then call again in a few days. Patience wasn't one of her strong suits, though. Pacing the hardwood floor over and over, Naomi weighed the pros and cons of heading over to Uncle Frank's house. He wouldn't want to see her either, but at least Naomi wasn't just wasting time, pacing and driving herself crazy. She needed to take action. She needed to try.

Glancing at herself in the hallway mirror, Naomi stopped and raked a hand through her hair. Movement from behind her appeared in the reflection. It was Nick, with a dark hood pulled over his face. Gasping, she spun to face him. As quickly as he had appeared, he was gone.

"I'm doing this so you can leave me alone. Let me take care of business without you scaring the crap out of me, Nick." She shook her head as Zelda arched her back and leapt out of sight, sideways up on four feet at once.

"And I know you can hear me." She grabbed her bag. "Wish me luck with your charming uncle."

As she stood, her hand placed on the doorknob, ready to leave, Naomi heard a door from the other room slam loudly. She still had the ability to piss him off. That could be good or bad. "Gotcha."

Naomi barely contained her grin as she made her way down the driveway. Getting into her car, Naomi pressed the power button on her cell phone and located the snapshot of Uncle Frank's address.

 Miriam would lose it if she knew what Naomi was up to. What Miriam Marty didn't know wouldn't hurt her. Naomi just wouldn't mention it unless something productive came out of this visit.

Her mind was on overdrive. Once upon a time, not so long ago, she had actually dated that monster of a ghost back at her house. She was ashamed to admit it, even to herself. Officer Marty had even accused her of being a poor judge of character back when they first met. Miriam had apologized many times over, but the fact remained that Naomi had been fooled by Nick's charm.

If she hadn't located Uncle Frank's street, she would still surely be reprimanding herself. "Let's see: 54 Palm Street . . ." Naomi muttered as she spied the modest white house.

"Cooperate with me, Frank. Let's make this easy on both of us." Speaking to herself was becoming more of a habit since all this crazy ghost business had begun.

Smoothing her top, Naomi cleared her throat and walked up the steps to Frank's home. The outdoors could stand a woman's touch. She figured the inside of the house would be equally bleak.

She knew that he was a single guy, that he had once married but it hadn't stuck. No surprise there.

Rapping on the door, Naomi bit down on her lip and waited. Nothing. There was no car in the driveway, but there was a garage. If he didn't answer in a minute, she would go and see if the garage was empty.

The door opened with a swift movement as Naomi gathered her thoughts. What was it she had planned to say first?

"Well, what do we have here?" Uncle Frank sneered as she stepped back, his small eyes scanning her up and down.

"Officer Frank." Mistake number one. How could she have addressed him like that? Damn, she knew he lost his job as a result of the cover-up, but he made her nervous.

Shaking his head, he blew out a harsh breath. "Nope. Thanks to you and your nosiness, I no longer have the pleasure of having that title or my career."

"I—er, Frank. I left you a message. We need to talk."

"In case you hadn't noticed, I didn't return your call. Now, where I come from, when someone doesn't call you back, that usually means they don't want to speak with that person."

He was pissing her off. She wasn't the criminal here, he was. "I'm not the one who broke the law. If I were you, I'd listen up and listen up good." Raising her voice, she seemed to get his attention.

He stared at her, not interrupting. "Now you can choose to believe this or not, but I'm here because I feel there's foul play involved in Nick's death." Realizing that she should have mentioned she was sorry about Nick's death, she quietly continued. "And I'm sorry to hear about Nick."

"I'm sure you've lost a lot of sleep over his death," Frank replied, his mouth a thin, tight line.

"Actually . . . I have." He had no idea how much sleep she had lost due to Nick's presence. "That's why I'm here. Nick came to me. Or rather, his spirit did."

His eyes popped wide. "What?"

"He's been haunting me. I figure he wants closure. And I also know that his death was not a suicide, nor was it an accident."

Frank laughed harshly, taking a large step back. "Now I suspected you were off your rocker before, but now it's been confirmed. You're bat shit crazy, aren't you, little girl?"

She closed in the space between them. "You're the one who's nuts. If you don't listen to me, you'll find out just how stupid you are to ignore me. Your nephew wants peace and he won't rest until I give it to him."

"I see. Okay, so let's just say this. I play along with your wild notions and then what? What exactly do you want from me and why the hell would Nick look to you, of all people, to help him? He couldn't stand the sight of you."

"It seems I have this ability—" Oh, this was ridiculous, standing here, trying to speak rationally about ghosts, especially to this poor specimen of a human being. "Forget it. What I need you to do is to go down to the police station and request that Nick's case be opened for suspicion of foul play."

Frank chuckled. "Me? They would laugh me right out of the station. Heck, I'd throw myself out if I could. Ain't gonna happen, little girlie."

"Okay, then fine, have it your way. Nick will never rest. He'll probably end up blaming you in the long run and I don't know how these things work but I'm pretty sure Nick can find his way to your home next."

"Now that's crazy talk. This is nuts." He continued to shake his head, but after a moment Frank's gaze was directed to Naomi and he no longer laughed. "Why me?"

"You know better than anyone the answer to that. You're his only living relative in the area. It has to be you. Do you really think I'm enjoying this little visit? I would give anything not to be here."

"They're going to laugh in my face. There's no point."

"Let them laugh. They have to consider the request. That's all I need from you. Officer Marty will take it from there."

Frank waved his hand through the air and stepped back into his house. Before he shut the door, he glanced at Naomi. "Yes. Good old Officer Marty. Tell her I said hi."

"You have all the charm of your nephew," Naomi muttered to the closed door.

Her visit hadn't gone as horribly as she had expected. She had a strong feeling that despite Frank's rudeness and hostility, he would be at the station soon, opening up the case.

Now that she had handled that crucial step, maybe she could get some writing time in. Jules was going to throw a fit if she didn't finish her story. Close—she was very close to giving her characters closure. Closure, but never rest, for her characters would be forever in her heart, a part of her soul. And the piece she enjoyed the most, of course, was sharing their lives with her readers.

Stepping on the gas, Naomi mentally calculated wrapping up the dramatic climax and closing for her story. She was so close to finishing and then she could focus her energy where it so desperately needed to be.

A call sounded from the car speakers as Naomi glanced at the screen on her dashboard. It was Bryce.

"Hey!" She was excited to share her news with Bryce regarding Uncle Frank.

"Hi, Naomi."

He sounded down. Knowing how upset he had been last night about Genna's return and the impact it might have on Holly's life, she sighed.

"You okay?" She lowered her voice.

"I'm fine."

She guessed otherwise, though. "It's Genna, isn't it?"

"Yes. I told you last night how upset Holly was."

Shoot. And she had promised to go over and speak with her. Her head was so wrapped up in Nick and her looming deadlines with her publishing company she had forgotten to stop over last night. Bryce's cool good night call should have clued her in to her misstep.

"I'm so sorry. I'm planning on stopping by today to speak with Holly as soon as she gets home from school." She felt awful. Naomi needed to prioritize and Bryce and Holly had to be on the top of her list, regardless of the paranormal events happening in her home.

"If you're too busy, that's fine. She'll understand."

Still, his tone was distant. "Now, why would you say that? I feel horrible about not stopping by. Not that it's an excuse, but Jules had been on me to finish my book and well, you know, with Nick and all . . ."

"Stop. I'm sorry. I know you have a lot going on as well. It's just getting to me. I feel powerless, you know?"

She didn't know from firsthand experience how it felt, but she could only imagine his feelings of helplessness.

"I understand. Please, tell me what I can do for you."

"Just be here. Be here for the both of us."

"Of course." And she would.

"Love you. I'll talk to you soon."

"Love you too, Bryce. I'll pop over and talk with Holly this afternoon, okay?"

"Sure. That would be nice."

Although Bryce had seemed to perk up a bit, Naomi cursed at herself. She knew she had disappointed him.

CHAPTER TWELVE

Bryce

TRUE TO HER word, Naomi had stopped by as soon as Holly had stepped off the bus. He was bummed that she had forgotten to come by as she had promised, the night before, but he also understood the pressure Naomi was under. They were all human. Now that she had been over to speak with Holly, his daughter's spirits were looking up and therefore, so were his own. Bryce almost felt as if things were back to normal until his cell phone beeped with an incoming text.

If you keep ignoring me, I'm stopping by.

Damn.

Placing his head in his hands, Bryce exhaled deeply.

Game time. He should have known. There was no ignoring Genna. He had never told her his address, but with technology at everyone's fingertips these days, it was no stretch to imagine how easily Genna could find them.

He had no clue where she was staying and didn't care to put forth the small effort to find out.

His fingertips grazed the keyboard of his phone but then he stopped himself. His lawyer had advised against putting anything in writing. Anything at all. So he gave in and called her.

Answering on the first ring, Genna's voice filled the air. It had been so long since he'd actually spoken with her.

"Well, it's about time."

"Genna. What can I do for you?"

"Why haven't you returned my calls? Why does it take threatening to stop by to finally get a response from you?"

So this was how it was going to be. Her snippy tone practically cried out for an argument. He wasn't biting. "I've been busy. What's going on?"

"*What's going on?* I'm here, like I told you."

"And?" But he already knew what her next words would be. He held his breath.

"*And*—I'd like to see my daughter."

He nearly laughed. *Her* daughter? Where had Genna been the past year? What kind of mother just up and left? The played-out thoughts filled his head once more.

"You have *got* to be kidding me."

"Do I sound like I'm joking?" Genna barked.

"No, but this is a joke. Heck, *you're* a joke, Genna. Do you have any idea what this is going to do to Holly, have you even considered that?" His heart pounded.

"What? How could it be bad for a little girl to see her own mother? That could only be a good thing."

That was a laugh. "Yeah, normally I would have to agree with you. But in your case? That could be the worst thing for her."

"That's not very nice, Bryce. If I were you, I'd watch your tone. I am the mother of your daughter, after all."

Another joke. "I'm going to speak with my lawyer. Until then, I'm not committing to anything."

"*Excuse me*? Have you mistaken me for an idiot? I know my rights and I'm entitled to see Holly. Now, you can make this easy or you can make it difficult. What's it going to be?"

Damn. She was right. Legally, he couldn't stop her from visiting with Holly. "What if I don't allow it?"

"Then I'll push past you screaming and kicking. Would you like Holly to witness that? Talk about stress. Or you know, I could just pick her up from school—"

"You wouldn't dare! Don't you confuse her." Bryce's mind was already on the next step—calling the school and his lawyer to see exactly what could be done short-term.

"I wouldn't, Bryce. I'm not an evil monster. But I *could.*"

"Give me a few days." That should be time enough to make his calls and figure something out.

"Nah. See, I'm in the area now so I figured I'd stop by."

Bryce was left standing, phone in hand, as Genna disconnected the call. Damn. Now what? His fingers scrambled to call his lawyer, but there was no answer. He glanced at the time on his cell and realized it was after five o'clock and the office was closed. He tried his lawyer's cell phone. No answer there either.

He knew what needed to be done. Sprinting up the steps, he called for Holly. "Holly! Holly!" There it was again. This time he swore he heard a light pounding sound right outside Holly's open bedroom door.

Bursting into her bedroom, a dark shadow came to view but then disappeared. It had been beside Holly, right *there*. His first thought had been to wonder if Nick's spirit had traveled here, to his own home. He opened his mouth, ready to ask if Holly had witnessed the same apparition, but stopped when he saw her pained expression. Naomi's talk of ghosts was getting to him. He had enough going on without imagining spirits at his own home.

"What's wrong, Daddy?" Her brown eyes melted his heart.

"Nothing. Nothing, sweetie." He made a mental note to get to bed earlier that night and catch up on his sleep. "I just thought it would be nice to go out, maybe get some ice cream." The conversation with Genna replayed in his mind. He had to move quickly.

Her face lifted at the mention of the snack. "Ice cream? Okay!"

"Come on." He grabbed her shoes and a light jacket, figuring he could put them on later, when he was away from the house. Scooping her up, he then took the stairs as quickly as he could without alarming her any further. He needed to stay out of the house as long as he could this evening. Maybe Genna would show her stubborn streak and wait them out, but at least there was the possibility that she would give up and go home, giving him the time he needed to contact his lawyer for advice.

He should have done this much earlier. Somehow he figured he had time on his side but now he knew how foolish his hesitation had been.

As Bryce opened the door to his house, he scanned the large driveway. So far, no sign of Genna. His fingers fumbled over the safety straps of Holly's car seat. *Get it together.*

Headlights came into view in the parking area just as he had snapped Holly's belt in place. The car gained speed as it approached. *Damn.*

There was no time to do anything but watch as Genna stepped out of her vehicle. The first thing he noticed was that she had cut her blonde hair. It was now a smooth bob. Her small stature did nothing to take away from her presence. Genna had always projected an air of confidence and self-righteousness. There was something off about her appearance though and he couldn't quite put his finger on what it was.

He had already closed the door on Holly's side of the car. Sticking his head inside the window, he assured Holly he would be back in a moment. Playing with her stuffed cat, Holly was blissfully unaware of the impending drama that was likely to unfold.

"Genna."

Her eyes scanned his body, from his head to his toes. "You're looking good. But then again, Bryce, you always have."

"What are you doing? Genna, I'm begging you to see reason. Give me time to prepare Holly for your visit. She's extremely vulnerable."

Genna walked forward and leaned her body so that she could catch a glimpse of Holly's back in the car seat. Holly's arms bounced up and down, holding her stuffed toy. *Please.*

Did he see a flicker of emotion pass over Genna's face? For a brief moment she seemed to ponder over his words.

"You win. This time. I want to see her, Bryce. But I don't want to hurt her. I'm her *mother*. I'm human. I made an awful mistake."

Was she human? "You sure did." But he breathed a sigh once he realized that she wouldn't bother Holly today.

"I know that, Bryce. Damn, don't you think I know? I'm trying hard, really hard, to straighten out my life. I'm in therapy, I'm getting help."

"Fine. Good for you, I'm happy to hear that. But I'm sure any therapist would tell you what harm your presence could do to Holly right now."

Her eyes misted over as she gazed up at Bryce. "I know that. I need her though. I need my daughter in my life. I was so, so wrong to leave her, to leave the both of you."

"But you did." He remained firm.

Genna didn't acknowledge his last words. "We had a family. A beautiful little family," she wept.

Tears flowed freely as Genna's eyes darted to Bryce's truck. He rarely recalled Genna crying, but he wasn't going to be sucked in.

"I think it's time for you to go now, Genna." He gently led her to her car door, hoping she would cooperate.

She stopped short of getting into her car and looked up at Bryce from her small height. "I'm going to make it up to the both of you, I promise."

He shook his head forcefully. "Just go."

"I miss this—her, and you too, Bryce."

Her expression held pain and sorrow, but Genna was a child when it came to maturity and her emotions. He felt nothing but pity for her.

"Go, Genna. We'll talk about Holly later."

Genna's eyes pleaded for him. She reached for his arm and held on. From the distance he saw a figure approaching in the darkness. Genna sensed his reaction and turned to look at the woman coming closer.

Naomi froze, taking in the scene before her. Genna's glance darted back and forth between Bryce and Naomi. *She knew.* Genna knew something was up.

"Who the hell is *that?*"

CHAPTER THIRTEEN

Naomi

AT FIRST, NAOMI wasn't sure who the woman was, but then as she drew closer, there was no doubt in Naomi's mind who was standing there. The way the other woman gazed up at Bryce, clutching his arm. Even in the dimly lit parking area, Naomi knew. It was Genna. It had to be.

Naomi wasn't prepared for her raw, tangled emotions. It was easy enough to imagine that Bryce had once been married, but it was entirely different altogether to witness another woman—make that a very attractive other woman—with her hands on Bryce.

She stood, frozen to the spot. Seeing Bryce watching her, she maintained eye contact until she saw the other woman turn, her eyes planted on Naomi. She shouldn't be here. This felt strange, wrong.

Spinning on her heels, she then stepped up the pace and headed for her front door. She didn't look back until she heard Bryce calling for her. Naomi waved to him, signaling it was okay. She would talk to him later. Bryce's hands dropped to his sides as he went back to face Genna.

It was fine. Bryce had informed Naomi of Genna's return. He was being completely upfront and honest with her. There was nothing to worry about. Nothing at all. She closed the door behind her and leaned against it, exhaling in her dark entrance foyer.

"What's the matter?"

Clutching her chest, Naomi screamed as she spied Nick standing in the shadows right in front of her. A screeching Zelda sped off, leaving Naomi to face this demon on her own. He had appeared horrid before, but now it was worse. His skin had grayed and shadows played under his eyes.

"You, you scared me," she managed. Of course he had frightened her.

"What else is wrong? Tell me." His footsteps pounded on the hardwood floor. *Don't touch me. Please.*

"Nothing. Well, this, actually. Stop sneaking up on me." Naomi tried to still her shaking hands. Between her near run in with Genna and now this, she was on the edge of losing it.

Eerie laughter filled every inch of the room. Naomi pulled her arms around her middle. Icy fingers tapped her shoulder. He was gone.

But the room maintained its chilly temperature. "Where are you? I asked you not to do this." Naomi peered around the dark room, making her way to the light switch several feet away.

In a flash, the frigid fingers returned, this time pulling her. "Stop!" He was messing with her head, attempting to scare the crap out of her. Her body slammed to the ground despite her efforts to repel him. He was too strong. Her aching, limp body pressed against the invisible form.

Nick's bitter tongue licked the outside of her ear. His breathing grew harsh as he continued licking across her face.

Stop. Stop. Shutting her eyes tightly, she knew she couldn't overpower him at this moment.

"Nick—"

She was losing this battle to him. She needed to think, gain her strength, but it was so hard with him holding her down with his dead weight.

"I want you to see how Maggie and Ryan felt—all of it. You made me into this untrusting mess. It's your fault," he hissed.

Swift hands pulled her head up and then smacked it down. Over and over again; her head felt hot, numb even. Opening her mouth to speak, Naomi's lame attempt was met with another thud.

Emptiness filled her core. She opened her mouth to scream but sound wouldn't come.

Then she saw it, or rather, felt it.

Again, the vision on the cliff. She faced Nick and Ryan, pushing between them. Hitting her head on a rock, she tasted blood. Her mouth dry as cotton, she tried to stand, but wooziness prevented her from righting herself. She stumbled again, tripping over a rock and then the long, dark descent as awareness hit. Her heart would cease beating in mere seconds. Worst of all were the screams, first her own, then Ryan's and Nick's. Seeing Ryan stumble over the cliff after her, she closed her eyes but couldn't erase the horrific image of Ryan's eyes open wide, and his mouth caught in a scream. It would be forever etched in her mind.

She knew this horrid scheme was playing out from Maggie's point of view, but Naomi was helpless to stop the images from bouncing continuously through her tired mind.

Then, something else. She was now on top of the cliff peering down over the edge. Maggie's body lay at the bottom of the cliff, torn like a ragdoll. She felt her stomach rise and vomited all over the wooded area.

But Ryan? Where was his body?

Deeper and deeper she was sucked into the dark, bottomless pit of despair. *Think. Think. Don't let him do this. He can't kill you. You're too strong.*

It was Bryce's voice she heard now. It gave her the strength she needed to climb out of the heavy darkness.

Gasping, Naomi slowly pulled herself up to a sitting position. Her mind registered the fact that her house was now at a normal temperature. Zelda sat beside her, rising to lick her face.

Nick. She was alone. But he had gone too far this time. Naomi had seriously thought she had this situation under control. She had doubted that he would physically harm her. Knocking her head on the floor crossed a new line, a dangerous one that she hoped never to revisit. For some sick reason, Nick got a kick out of seeing Maggie's and Ryan's deaths play out time and again in Naomi's mind.

Reaching a hand up to soothe her sore head, Naomi startled as the room lost heat. Zelda let out a shrill cry as she headed out of the room.

No. Not so soon.

This time, a gentle breeze lifted her hair as something brushed at her cheek. It was a mere whisper. So faint she almost missed it.

He wants his thoughts out of his head. They're driving him insane. Settle it. Settle it before you go mad.

"Who's that?" Naomi rose to her feet, stumbling slightly. She held her throbbing head in her hands.

She was gone. But she had been there moments before.

Even as quiet as her message had been, Naomi recognized the voice and this time she understood her words clearly. She could hardly forget.

"Maggie," Naomi cried out in the empty room.

IT COULD HAVE been hours.

It could have been minutes.

Naomi had no idea how much time had gone by since she had left Bryce standing outside in the lot with his ex-wife by his side. It seemed like a lifetime ago. But now, here he was, sitting at the table beside her. An exuberant Holly could be heard inside the living room playing with Zelda.

"Let me see your head." Bryce parted her hair, gently soothing her sore head.

"I'm okay." But was she really? Naomi was exhausted, both mentally and physically.

"I could kill him."

Naomi chuckled harshly. "He's already dead."

The moment wasn't lost between them. Their laughter filled the air for the briefest instant and it felt good to laugh, even for a second.

"I'm so sorry you had to see Genna."

She couldn't think about Genna right now. She had more pressing concerns, namely Nick and the fact that he could have killed her moments earlier.

"Bryce, it's fine. Please—I don't want to talk about this. I don't feel like talking about anything. Just be here for me, okay?" Her eyes pleaded with him.

"You're right. That's nothing compared to what just happened to you, I just thought—"

"No. It's not that it's nothing. I don't want to think. Not about Genna, not about Nick. The only thing that I want right now is to be here with you, keeping me safe."

Thoughts of Holly playing in the next room intensified her worry but Bryce had said they would be leaving soon. Naomi couldn't even consider the idea of Holly being harmed.

Bryce shook his head. "I'm helpless here. It kills me that I can't protect you. Nobody can help you and that's probably the most awful feeling I can think of."

"You're wrong. Maggie was here, I told you. She's trying to warn me."

"But can she protect you?"

"Not enough, from what it would appear." It was a fact. Nick could have killed her and it would have been too late. Surely Maggie—and Ryan, for that matter—would rescue her in a heartbeat if they could. Of that she was one hundred percent certain.

"Speed it up, Naomi. Do what it takes and then come back to me, all of you. I need you."

His words brought her to tears. Nick was intruding on a beautiful thing she had going with Bryce. He was taking away her precious time, time that was needed to nurture her new family.

"Don't cry, honey." Bryce pulled her close. "Just be here with me."

"I am here. Stop saying that." He got on her nerves when he spoke like that. But she knew what he meant.

He kissed Naomi gently and nodded toward the living room.

"Holly! Time to go." Bryce called for his daughter.

Smiling at the sight of Holly bounding into the room with a delighted Zelda in her arms, she felt warmth and peace.

"Call me later?" She wanted to speak more about Genna, after her head had cleared a bit. She wrapped her arms around Bryce and Holly before they went out for their ice cream.

"Sure you don't want to join us?" Bryce offered.

"Nah, I'm beat. Have some quality time with Holly."

"Night, Mommy."

Her heart quickened at the use of Holly's new name for her. She didn't know if it was right or wrong that Holly called her Mommy. Not when she had a mother who was now coming back into the picture. It felt right, though, and if it made Holly happy to call her Mommy, then it made Naomi happy, too.

"Night, sweetie." She bent down and placed another kiss atop Holly's tiny head.

Bryce's gaze lingered a moment before he cleared his throat. She couldn't place the emotion that had been written on his face.

Naomi waited a moment before walking into the living room. It would be an early night.

"Zelda. What do you say we watch an old movie for a bit?" Naomi grabbed the remote and scooped Zelda into her arms. Minutes into the movie, Naomi drifted into a fitful sleep.

Tonight her dreams centered around Bryce, Holly, and unfortunately, Genna.

CHAPTER FOURTEEN

Naomi

WAKING WITH A splitting headache, Naomi stretched her arms over her head. Flashes of her dream from last night came to mind. In her dream, Bryce had decided it was best for Holly, best for *his* family, if he and Genna reunited. And there was more—a raven-haired woman had appeared before her, so young and stunningly beautiful, she had stolen her breath. None of this made sense, not the random blue-eyed spirit, nor the images of Bryce and Genna. Madness swirled around her, day and night it seemed. It hadn't felt like a dream, not at all. Her heart had actually grieved so much she woke with fresh tears on her pillow.

But it wasn't real and Bryce would never do that. If Naomi thought for one minute it was the best thing for him and Holly, she would have no choice but to step aside.

NAOMI

Genna wasn't a good mother, that much was clear. She had serious flight risk potential and in Naomi's opinion, she could never be trusted again. At least that was what Naomi believed to be true. There was also the fact that Bryce claimed he and Genna had fallen out of love before Holly's mom had decided to take off with another man.

Was Nick behind these dreams as well?

Another form of torment for her?

Or was it her own mind torturing herself this time? Most likely, it was Naomi's worries coming to surface. Ever since she had seen Genna with her own eyes the night before, Bryce's ex hadn't been far from her mind.

She was worrying needlessly, that was all. But she would feel better after speaking with Bryce directly. Checking her cell phone on the small table beside the couch, Naomi bit her lip as she saw the missed call from last night. She had fallen asleep watching the movie and had missed Bryce's call.

Pressing Bryce's name on her cell phone, she waited for him to pick up but then heard the beep that signaled he was on another call. She continued another moment before he picked up.

"Hey. Can I call you back in a few? I'm on the line."

"Sure. Take your time."

"Ugh, it's Holly's mother again. I'll call you back as soon as I can."

Holly's mother.

Again.

It's fine. She was going to have to deal with this and she figured it must be far worse for Bryce. She would be patient. Patient and understanding.

Naomi made a fresh pot of coffee as she opened and closed the door to the refrigerator for the third time in a row. She wasn't hungry.

The combination of her pounding head and her dream from the night before had made her mood sour. Reaching into the cabinet next to her sink for the ibuprofen, she fumbled with the vitamins trying to reach the bottle.

Her head would feel better soon and hopefully the rest would follow. On her agenda today was a visit to see Mr. and Mrs. Field. First she would call Miriam to see if Frank had stopped by the station yet.

A vision stopped her short. Bryce's smiling face followed by Holly lifting her arms toward her in a sunny field. Flowers bloomed and she reached to pick an impossibly bright yellow one. Holly was looking at something off in the distance. It was Bryce. He smiled widely, he looked peaceful. From behind him, a stunning Genna appeared, catching up to Bryce and clasping his hand. Holly's bright smile blinded Naomi, causing her to turn her head to the side, just for a moment. The little girl then spun around and ran, right into the arms of her mother and father. A happy family, together at last.

No. Naomi cradled her head, the incessant pounding making her nauseous.

No. She tried to stop her body from shaking. *Nick, don't do this. I know this isn't real. I know this isn't happening.*

Sitting down, she took a deep breath and scanned the kitchen for signs of Nick. "You bastard. Don't you dare play head games with me. He loves me and you can't take that away from me." But was this Nick at play or was she slowly losing her mind? Could it be some type of breakdown from all the recent stress?

She fiddled with her cell, finding Miriam's number despite her quaking hands.

"Miriam. Any news with Frank?" She found her voice.

"As a matter of fact, he did stop by. I'm going to ignore the fact that you went over there against my wishes only because the case is now officially opened. You must be some kind of miracle worker. What did you say to him?"

"Just that his nephew was haunting me and he might be next." Naomi laughed and she realized that it felt good. She stood to prepare her coffee, rubbing her temples.

"Oh is that all? Well, whatever you did, it worked. Now I have to try to figure this thing out. You don't happen to know who Nick's doctor was, do you?

"Um—yes."

Neither spoke for a moment.

"Why the pause? What did you do, Naomi?" Her harsh tone discouraged Naomi from offering up too much.

"I just switched doctors for a day, that's all," Naomi squeaked into her phone.

"Okay, I don't even know what that means and I don't think I want to. Give it to me, bottom line."

"Well, his name is Dr. Bender."

"*Dan* Bender?"

"I'm pretty sure that's his first name. Anyway, I think the good doctor might have given Nick painkillers. I mean, it's just a guess, and I'm not getting good vibes from him. The way I figure it, Nick most likely became addicted and then kept obtaining refills—"

"Whoa, girl. Slow down. Slow *way* down. First of all, Dr. Bender is highly respected in the community of doctors *and* in this town."

Naomi rolled her eyes. "So I've heard."

"*And* if I may go on, Dan Bender plays golf with Phil and they're becoming pretty good friends."

Ryan's brother Phil had recently moved to town after Ryan's death. The brothers hadn't been particularly close the last few years and Naomi suspected that Phil felt some lingering guilt. It was no surprise that coupled with those feelings and the fact that he and Miriam were growing closer by the day, he rented out a small apartment on the outskirts of town.

"Wonderful," Naomi muttered. "It seems that everyone in town is impressed with Dr. Bender except for me."

"Listen, Naomi. Stay out of it now, hear me? I'm the police officer and I'll take it from here."

"With all due respect, I'm the one who is being tormented by Nick until this is resolved, so excuse me if I'm trying to speed things up. Oh, and by the way, Nick tried to kill me yesterday."

"What?!"

"You heard me. I'll try not to step on your toes too much, but I believe past experience proves that we work much better together."

"He tried to *kill you?*"

"I'm not sure if that was his intention, but he certainly could have. I have the bruises on my head to prove it."

"Hell, Naomi. I'm sorry."

"Not your fault."

"Agreed, but let's nail this sucker that killed him and send Nick off to a place where he can never bother you again."

"I'm in."

Naomi's thoughts were back to Nick as she ended her call to Miriam and headed out to see Maggie's parents. It was odd that Maggie reached over from the other side to give her a message yesterday. She was under the impression that now that Maggie had achieved the peace that she was so desperately seeking, she wouldn't hear from her again.

Baffled as usual about the paranormal, Naomi supposed Maggie had sensed she was in danger and crossed over because of their bond. Could Ryan do the same? She knew in her heart that he would if he had the power to.

So Nick wished to transfer all the horror to her mind so that he could gain serenity? There was no way she would take on or share the burden of his experiences and actions. No way in hell. Suspicion that he also wished to torment her in the worst way possible, just for kicks, also filled her mind. He was that kind of guy.

As she pulled into the Fields' driveway, Naomi was hit with another flash. This time Bryce and Genna snuggled on the couch, with Holly in between them. So he had the power to reach her outside of her home. Or again, was this all her? Heck, she couldn't tell the difference anymore, the lines blurred between the paranormal and her reality. Was there even a difference anymore?

Naomi knew she was stronger than this, stronger than him. She just had to pull it together.

She wondered how she could beat Nick at his own game.

SEEING MR. AND Mrs. Field was always bittersweet. Naomi thought their visit had gone well and she loved seeing them, but would there be a time when they could all just enjoy their little visits and not be reminded of all the sorrow that cut Maggie's life short?

NAOMI

Miriam had texted that she and Phil would be having drinks and dinner at the local Italian place in town later and wanted to know if Naomi and Bryce would join them. The restaurant was her favorite and Holly was going to visit with her aunt this evening.

Why not?

She hated to admit it, but the few times she had seen Phil, it felt funny. Phil had settled things back home after Ryan's death and then returned shortly back East. It was because he reminded her so much of Ryan, that must be it.

The times she had been beside Phil in the past, it was almost as if Ryan himself was seated across from her, laughing, smiling and, well, living. From Phil's voice to his dark blue eyes, it was all Ryan. But not. She and Phil didn't share the bond or the love she had known with Ryan. There were no memories with Phil, only reminders of a beautiful, selfless man she would never see again. Phil was also quieter, not full of passion for life. It wasn't fair to compare the two, but Naomi found herself doing just that each time they met.

She would text Bryce and see if he was game. Besides, maybe she could casually bring up the topic of Dr. Bender.

The more she thought about it, the more she considered that the doctor might be somehow involved. He was a sketchy one and her gut cried out that Dan Bender wasn't all he appeared.

CHAPTER FIFTEEN

Bryce

"I DON'T KNOW. I feel like he's not the person he appears, you know? I feel like there's more to Dr. Bender than meets the eye."

Phil cocked his head to the side. "I'm not sure I'm following you."

"Oh, you know how writers' minds work. Way too curious if you ask me," Miriam commented, eyeing Naomi. Bryce eyed her warily as well.

Was it the glass of wine Naomi was sipping?

There was something up with Naomi tonight and from the daggers that her friend had been sending her the past half hour, Bryce knew that Miriam felt it too.

Questions. She was playing it off like she was just making casual conversation, but Bryce knew her too well. He also knew where this preoccupation with Dr. Bender stemmed from.

Trouble could only come from her line of questioning. Geez, Naomi mentioned that Phil and Dr. Bender were becoming friendly. He made a mental note to mention that she was crossing the line of being impolite with Phil.

"Curious? Call it a gut feeling—"

"Okay, honey. I think we should drop the subject, huh?" He rubbed her thigh from his seat beside her.

"I happen to like Dan. I mean, what's not to like?" Phil studied Naomi from across the table.

"What's not to like? You're joking, right?" Naomi spoke up.

Naomi wiggled in her seat as Bryce watched Miriam's smug expression from across the table. She had kicked Naomi under the table, something he had considered but knew only a female friend could get away with.

"Hey!" Naomi winced.

"I think someone needs to slow down on that wine there," Miriam sneered.

Phil's expression remained neutral but he shifted uncomfortably in his seat. "Perhaps it would be best if we discussed something else. How's your new book going, Naomi?" Phil asked.

"Oh, I'm wrapping it up and on a tight deadline but due to unforeseen distractions, I'm cutting it pretty close."

Another swift kick from Miriam.

"Ouch!"

Bryce cleared his throat. "Um, how was *your* day, Miriam?"

"*My* day was perfect. Thank you for asking."

Naomi sulked as she grabbed for her wine. What had gotten into her? He knew she was stressed, but his was out of character for her. Minutes ticked by and the conversation flitted from one topic to another, and all the while, Naomi remained silent as she sipped at that damn glass of wine.

"Naomi? Feel like getting some fresh air for a minute?" Bryce stood and held his hand out to her. Luckily, she reached for it and followed him out of the restaurant.

Once they were outside and safely out of hearing distance from Miriam and Phil, Bryce asked what was bothering her.

"I have this feeling. I know that Dr. Bender is somehow involved. Either directly or indirectly, but I'm going to find out."

"How much coffee have you had today?" Bryce waited out her pause.

"I don't know, a few cups."

"And when was the last time you ate?"

She glanced down at the ground, shifting her feet. "Not since breakfast."

"Just as I thought. You really shouldn't drink wine on an empty stomach. And how much sleep did you get last night?"

She lifted her gaze to meet his, jutting out her jaw. "Well, let's see, *Dad*. In between nightmares of Nick and then you and Genna?" She paused dramatically. "Probably an hour or two?"

Ignoring the *Dad* jab, Bryce sucked in his breath. "Geez, Naomi. Why didn't you just say you were too tired to go out tonight? That would have been fine with me. Hell, it would have been better than this." He spread his hands out, gesturing toward the restaurant.

"What's wrong with *this?*"

She knew what was wrong, dammit. She was pushing his buttons.

"You've been grilling that poor guy for half the night about his friend."

"Isn't that a bit dramatic? Half the night?" Naomi laughed bitterly.

Bryce's stomach tightened as he was reminded of the ugly spats he and Genna had shared. Too many to count. This was all wrong, He and Naomi should have just stayed home tonight.

"Well?" Her hands rested on her hips, her eyes challenging him.

"You know what? If you don't stop, I'm going to leave. I have enough going on right now without this."

"Oh, really. And I don't?" Naomi stepped closer, hands still on her hips.

Who was this person and what was happening here? Genna was hounding him day and night the past few days. He hadn't shared half of it with Naomi because he didn't want to upset her. Strange occurrences at his own home continued to taunt him, just out of sight. His emotions were wound so tightly right now. Genna swore she was a changed woman, Holly was constantly asking where her mom was, but she was referring to Naomi, not Genna.

The last thing he would consider would be getting back with Genna, but she wasn't letting up and the situation was going to get downright ugly before it got any better.

Taking hold of her wrists, he gently pressed down. He needed her to calm down before the unwelcome emotions took a stronger hold over him. "Stop Naomi, just stop. Please." He silently prayed this nonsense would end.

But then Naomi's tears spilled. "I can't take this."

"What? Talk to me."

"This—Nick, Genna . . . I can't eat, I can't sleep."

"I told you not to let this consume you. I knew—"

He realized the second the words escaped that he shouldn't have spoken them aloud.

"And how exactly would you like me to relax with Nick trying to destroy me? He's driving me crazy, filling my head with all of his darkness, all his evil."

"I'm sorry." He smoothed her hair back, but she pulled away.

"And Genna? Part of me wonders if she is a changed woman, if you and Holly would be better off back with her. That's her *mother*, Bryce."

"Naomi? Listen here. In my mind, in my opinion, *you're* Holly's mother. *You. Only you.*" He bit back tears of his own.

Naomi just shook her head, staring across the street at her house, only a short distance away.

"I need some time alone, Bryce. "

"What are you talking about? Where are you going?"

She ignored him, crossing the dark road that led to the field surrounding her house. She was acting crazy— what was he missing here?

"You can't just walk away!" he cried out, his arms high in the air. She didn't even glance back.

He could have gone after her. He should have.

But something held him back.

AFTER FINISHING THE awkward dinner with Miriam and Phil, Bryce walked across the same field, but turned in the direction of his own home. He didn't need this stress, either. What they both needed was some time to think.

Some room to breathe.

Perhaps in the morning light, things would look different. Bryce tried to clear his mind of Naomi as he picked up Holly from her aunt's house and later put her to bed. Naomi occupied his thoughts as he reached for his cell phone and then placed it down with a soft thud.

He loved her. But he couldn't stand speaking with her right now, not with the way she had behaved earlier.

But she was part of his soul. If he didn't help her somehow, he could lose her forever and that wasn't something he planned on doing.

His cell rang just as he drifted off. In his groggy state, he assumed it would be Naomi so he answered, eager to hear her voice right now.

"Naomi."

"Ah, no. It's me."

He felt as if had been punched in the gut.

"Genna, it's late."

"I know, Bryce. I'm scared."

"What is it?" Bryce sat up straight in his bed.

"I don't think I've ever felt so alone. I messed up, so badly. I miss you guys so much it hurts."

"Genna—"

"I know. I know you're engaged. I realize that you're happy with this—"

"Naomi. Her name is Naomi."

"Whatever. My point is that we have history, we're a family."

"*Were* a family. We *were* a family, Genna. That's past tense."

"But can't you see that we can be again? Open your mind to the possibilities. Think about the good times we shared, you and me and then with Holly."

"We fell out of love and you lost my trust, Genna. My trust for you with Holly as well."

"I'll wait. Play around with what's-her-name and then come home to me."

He stared at his phone as she disconnected the call. It was almost worse when Genna didn't yell and scream.

Play around with what's-her-name.

Did Genna have any clue that true love was loving someone so much you were willing to put your own needs to the side for the sake of another? Take the good and the bad?

Genna had no clue, but he did.

Glancing at the late time on his digital clock, Bryce wanted nothing more than to go to Naomi right now. But he couldn't leave Holly, of course. Tomorrow, he would go over to her house and hold her until the hurt dissipated.

CHAPTER SIXTEEN

Bryce

AS BRYCE HAD promised himself, he had woken early the next morning to pay Naomi a visit. Holly was still at her dance lesson right up the road and he wasn't due to pick her up for another hour. This gave Bryce just enough time to pop in on Naomi. Thoughts had consumed his mind during the night making sleep just out of reach.

He sincerely hoped Naomi was in a better frame of mind than she had been last night. If not, well, then he would just have to deal with it. Either way, he had an idea that just might ease Naomi's recent tension. If he could arrange a few things, his plan just might work.

By the look on Naomi's weary face when she appeared at the door, it was evident that she hadn't found sleep the night before either.

"More bad dreams?" Bryce ventured, gazing into her bloodshot eyes.

"Well good morning to you, too." Naomi gestured for him to follow her inside and led the way into the kitchen. A fresh pot of coffee was brewing. He considered commenting on her recent caffeine habit but thought better of it. Besides, he could use a cup of coffee right now also.

"Mind if I have a cup, too?" He pointed toward the steaming coffee pot.

Naomi narrowed her eyes at him. "Are you sure you should? I mean, it's a tough habit to break. I should know."

Instantly, he grabbed her arm and pulled her close. "Don't, Naomi. Don't do this." His stomach turned again at the familiar feeling of arguing. He may not have been able to repair his broken relationship with Genna, but that was largely due to the fact that he didn't wish to make things right between them. This was different. He wouldn't let his relationship with Naomi deteriorate. Not when they truly loved one another. It was Nick screwing with her mind. This wasn't the Naomi he had grown to know, and he wasn't giving up on her.

Surprisingly, Naomi clung to Bryce and sobbed into his shoulder. "I'm sorry. I'm so sorry. I was such a witch last night." He didn't feel words were necessary, so he just grabbed Naomi and let her weep.

After her sobs subsided and her breathing became steady once more, he pulled himself back and looked into her eyes. It broke his heart to see her in so much pain.

"Don't be sorry. Just beat him, Naomi. You can do it, I know you can. You're a strong woman. The strongest I've ever known." He meant every word he said. She had the power to overcome Nick, she just needed to be brave enough to believe in herself and conquer that evil presence with all she was worth.

"I'm not so sure anymore. He's killing me, Bryce. Slowly, one night at a time. I can't sleep, I can barely eat these past few days." Tears rose in her eyes once more. He pulled her in and kissed her wet eyelashes. If he could take this pain from her and make it his own, he would do it in an instant.

"You, Naomi, are a force to be reckoned with. Stay strong." Naomi was, simply put, the strongest person he had ever come across.

Together they stood, clinging to each other. For a moment it was just the two of them again, the way it had been before Nick's spirit had tried to separate them. The more he thought this through, the more Bryce considered the fact that Nick was hitting Naomi low, where it hurt the most—her heart. Surely Nick knew how close they were, and what better way to torture Naomi than to break her heart? Nick was in for a serious wake-up call if he thought his devious scheme would work.

Zelda's mew broke the spell and forced them back to the present. It was as a switch had been turned; Naomi backed away and Bryce knew she was back in that dark, lonely place.

"Sweetheart—"

"I—It's so real, Bryce. These vivid dreams, I can't seem to separate the dreams from reality at times. You keep telling me it's okay and then Genna's image consumes me. Her voice, I know what her voice sounds like and I've never met her. How could that even be possible?"

"I really don't think it's her actual voice you're hearing. I mean, that's impossible. You were too far away that night in the lot to hear her voice clearly."

"It's smooth as silk."

That caught his attention. Genna did, in fact, have a very smooth and sultry voice. "That's just a guess."

"I *knew* it. She does, doesn't she? Wait, do you have any messages on your phone from her?'

Sure, he was certain that he had a few. When they had first divorced, his lawyer had advised keeping as many as possible because they may be needed as evidence at some point.

"I do have some I saved under the advice of my lawyer, but—"

"But what? Give it up." Naomi's arm extended toward him.

Thinking this through, Bryce wasn't sure it was the best idea to have Naomi listen to his ex pleading to get back together with him.

"Listen. I can handle it. Just hand me the phone, Bryce. It's important."

Begrudgingly, he acquiesced and grabbed his cell from his pants pocket. "Please remember that I don't feel the same way she does. I don't want her back." He didn't have to say the words, she should have known, but Bryce also knew that Naomi was in a tenuous place right now. He sighed, finding one of the saved messages before handing it over.

Without responding, Naomi grabbed the phone and placed her ear to it. Bryce clenched his jaw as he watched her fragile reaction to not only Genna's voice, but to her unsettling words as well. Fresh tears came to her eyes as she forced her hand toward him, returning the phone. Damn, the message he selected had been an old one, and therefore the least hurtful, in his opinion.

"Naomi—"

"It's her voice."

"I, I knew it wasn't a great idea for you to listen to that. It was a while ago, when she first left." Genna hadn't even been pleading for his attention then, if he remembered correctly; she had just stated that she would always love both him and Holly but that she had to follow her heart right now.

"Well, then I can only imagine what's she's saying now."

"Don't—"

Naomi's face clouded with emotion. He knew she was struggling, trying not to sink into Nick's trap. Finally, she spoke up. "Forget it. I don't care what that woman has to say right now. Don't you see what this means?"

"I wish I knew." He was struggling with the concept of Nick having the ability to plant Genna's voice inside of Naomi's head.

"He's more powerful than I had anticipated." She turned her head away from him.

Normally, Bryce figured he was pretty good at finding the words to comfort people he cared for. Not this time. What could he possibly say to make things right here? But then he remembered his idea from last night. It couldn't hurt.

"I was thinking about something earlier. I figure we could both use a break right about now."

She turned to face him. It was a start.

"What do you say about getting away for a night or two? Just the two of us, maybe head to the beach?"

Shaking her head, Naomi bit down on her lip. "No shot. I have a deadline. Jules would never understand."

"What good are you in this condition? And didn't you say you were almost finished with this book?'

"Almost. But I have another day or so of work to put on the finishing touches." He could see from the drop of her jaw that she was softening toward the idea.

"Tell you what, how about we go for two nights and during the day I'll leave you completely alone until you finish your book? A change of scenery might be just what you need right now."

Naomi nodded her head. "Okay, that just might work. But what about Holly? Doesn't she have school?"

"She has a long weekend, there were some unused snow days in the school calendar. We could all go, our first family trip. What do you say?"

"What about you? Mark wouldn't mind?"

Mark was Bryce's supervisor and he had been urging Bryce to take a long-needed vacation for a while now. "Mark is practically begging me to take some time off. Do you know how long it's been since I've taken more than a morning off?"

She was definitely warming to the idea. "Yes. Yes, that sounds amazing. The more that I think about it, the more I think it's a great idea. Do you think he could reach me there? That far away?" Her thoughts echoed his own. He figured anything was possible but he wasn't about to voice his concern.

"Nah. Maybe he needs a break, too."

Her lighthearted chuckle warmed him. There she was. That was the girl he knew. "Come here, you." He wrapped his arms around her slender frame. "Now get ready. I'm going to pick up Holly from dance and then make a few calls. I doubt it'll be hard to find a place this time of year." He had just the place in mind.

During the summer months, Cape Florence was a bustling destination, but in the springtime it shouldn't be too difficult to get a room.

Standing on her tiptoes, Naomi reached up and kissed him on his mouth. "Thank you."

"You bet. Now, start packing and figure we'll head out in a few hours. I have some work plans to settle with Mark, but it shouldn't be too long. Call me if you need me." Feelings of anxiety arose each time he left her the past few days. Anything could happen when it came to Nick and it frightened him to let his mind wander.

"What if?" Naomi grabbed his collar.

"What?"

"What if he does follow us there? What about Holly?"

"Naomi. If anything out of the ordinary happens, we'll head back, okay? I have a feeling we'll be fine, though." Call it intuition, but he believed that this break was exactly what they all needed.

CHAPTER SEVENTEEN

Naomi

OF COURSE HE was right. Bryce couldn't have picked a better time for all of them to take off and spend some quality time together. Naomi planned on working all day tomorrow while Bryce and Holly enjoyed the historic seaside village. Cape Florence was rich in history, being one of the country's oldest vacation spots dotted with gorgeous Victorian homes and buildings. Naomi also knew the area was rumored to be among the most haunted destinations in the country. That may not be exactly what she needed right now, but Naomi's interest was piqued.

"Did you know that Cape Florence is one of the most haunted towns in America?" Naomi whispered after looking over her shoulder at Holly, who was fast asleep.

She could have burst from laughter as his expression went from a smile to disbelief. "You're kidding, Please tell me you're kidding."

"Nope. And I can't believe you didn't know that." She was enjoying this, riling him up a bit.

"Seriously? Naomi, don't mess with me. Tell me you're joking." Gazing at his pained expression, she had to admit she felt a tad sorry for him.

When Bryce had mentioned the beach, it hadn't crossed her mind that he was considering Cape Florence. But honestly, it was perfect. Cape Florence held a special place in her heart. Her grandparents had once owned a home right off of the larger section of town, in the quiet sleepy section of the Cape. She had spent many a summer vacationing in the area, splashing in the waves on the small stretches of the local beach by her grandparents' home. Hours had been spent walking the several miles by beach into the more populated city area of the Cape. Never once had she encountered an otherworldly spirit, but then again her mind hadn't been open to the experience, and in her opinion, Maggie had been her gateway to the paranormal.

Naomi shook her head, biting back a grin.

Bryce's mouth dropped as he took his eyes from the road once more. "What's the matter with me? Hey, we can go somewhere else? There's plenty of beach towns on the way."

"I wouldn't have it any other way. Did I ever tell you about my childhood years spent vacationing in Cape Florence?"

One of the things that had initially attracted Naomi to Bryce was the fact that he listened to her eagerly and engaged her in conversation. They spoke at length not only about her memories of the Cape, but his own travels to the seaside town as well as some other vacation spots he had been to.

Comfortable silence now filled the air as Naomi sat back and closed her eyes, mentally savoring this time with Bryce and Holly. Just as she started nodding off, Holly woke, bright and cheerful. She was beside herself with excitement over this trip.

"Hi, baby," Bryce called out as he glanced at Holly from the rearview mirror.

"Hi, sweetie." Naomi turned to tickle Holly's knee. A particular memory came to her then, washing over her with warm emotion.

"Hey, do you know that my grandmother and I used to sing a song every time we drove down to Cape Florence together?" She could almost see her grandma seated beside her, hands on the steering wheel of her beloved compact car, singing with her, teaching her the lyrics to the song about the Cape.

"Really? Can we? Can we sing it too?"

She caught Bryce stealing a glance at her as he reached for her hand and squeezed it. Pressing down on his hand, she figured she had never been happier than she was at this moment.

There it was, that unmistakable scent. The smell of the ocean in the distance heightened her memory and the words to their song came back to her. "Okay, so it goes like this . . ."

THREE HOURS LATER, they had reached their destination. Pointing here and there, Naomi felt as if she were the child as they drove through town. How could she have forgotten how much this place meant to her? Already, only minutes in town, she felt her tension lessen. Feeling lighter than she had in months, Naomi sat up straighter in her seat. Inspiration to finish up her book would come easily, she thought. She couldn't wait to sink her teeth in and tidy up the loose ends. Then she could focus all her time and energy on Bryce and Holly.

There was a slight chill in the air as they stepped out of the truck. Stretching her arms out in front of her, Naomi yawned as she viewed the stunning bed and breakfast facing them.

"This is where we're staying?" Taking in the sprawling Victorian inn, Naomi grinned widely.

"This is our home for the next two nights. Jane's Ending," Bryce said. Naomi followed his gaze to the swinging sign detailed with a drawing of a closed book.

A chill coursed through Naomi as she stood, rooted to the spot. Peering out at the ocean across the street, Naomi considered the feeling could be due to the sea breeze, which had now picked up in intensity. She shivered, wrapping her arms around herself. It could be the breeze, of course. But then her eyes were drawn to the top window of the grand building and she could have sworn she saw the slight parting of a curtain.

"You okay?" Bryce squinted his eyes. "Honey?"

It took a moment before she realized he had spoken. "Ah, yes. All's good." Naomi forced a smile and reached in the back seat for Holly while Bryce grabbed their bags.

"This is so pretty!"

"Yes, Holly. And we'll have a fun time." Naomi tightened her grip on Holly's hand and followed Bryce up the long pathway to the front entrance.

Again, Naomi glanced up at the breathtaking inn and sighed as she avoided looking toward the window settled way up high. Most likely it was a worker, or perhaps a guest wandering around. From the look of the nearly empty parking area, not too many visitors were actually staying here at the moment.

"What's the matter?" Bryce stepped up his pace to meet her.

"Nothing. I'm just appreciating the amazing architecture."

"She's a beauty, that's for sure." He nodded in agreement. "Come on, let's get settled in and then we can explore a bit."

As beautiful as the outside of the bed and breakfast was, the inside didn't disappoint. Decorative touches that blended the seaside theme adorned the expansive walls. High arched ceilings gave way to a grand spiral stairway. Naomi watched as Holly's mouth opened wide, appreciating the beauty of the lobby and accompanying sitting room.

"Wow." Bryce's gaze turned to the staircase.

"I can't wait to explore this place," Naomi mumbled under her breath.

"And I hope you love every inch."

Startled by the woman's voice, Naomi jumped at the intrusion to her thoughts. Facing her was a pretty, blonde–haired woman. Naomi could have laughed out loud at Bryce's attempt to avoid staring at her. Despite the fact that this curvy blonde probably turned heads wherever she went, she seemed very sweet and down to earth as she went about checking them in.

"There. That should do it. I hope you guys have a great time. I'm Kristen, by the way. If you need anything, anything at all, just ring me. You guys are one of the few guests we have tonight, so please, don't hesitate to ask for anything. I'm practically begging for human interaction." The woman laughed heartily.

The last sentence made Naomi take notice, and was it her imagination that the woman glanced away nervously after speaking? What an odd way to verbalize the fact that the inn was empty. Human interaction? What other type of interaction would there be here? Her mind was at the upstairs window once more. The spirits were getting to her, even miles away. *Get a grip.*

"Oh, was that one of the guests wandering about upstairs a few minutes ago?"

"Come again?" Kristen's eyebrows shot upward as her hands stilled.

"The woman—there was a woman looking out the window upstairs. She looked a bit like you I suppose, but different." This woman's face appeared to be a bit more slender and at quick glance her hair looked longer, wavier.

"Oh, yes. I almost forgot. I was up there doing some quick cleaning and then I saw you guys and hurried down."

"But—" Naomi turned to point at the staircase. It would have been nearly impossible to travel downstairs in that short amount of time. Besides, she was pretty sure the woman was not Kristen.

Kristen waved a dismissive hand. "When you've lived here for a while, believe me, you get used to this big place. I can come downstairs in practically no time." Her bubbly laughter put Naomi at ease a bit.

"Sure, okay." Naomi glanced at Bryce and he seemed perfectly comfortable with her explanation. Maybe her memory was a bit off; she had, after all, only seen a quick flash of the person upstairs.

"Your room is just down the main hallway to the left, room number three. It's a suite, large enough for you all to spread out a bit, and the view is spectacular."

They thanked Kristen and made their way down the hallway. Holly zoomed ahead, intent on finding the room first.

"She's pretty, huh?"

"What, who, that lady? Oh, I guess. Didn't really notice."

Naomi stepped to his side and giggled. "Liar," she whispered into his ear as she playfully swatted him.

TOSSING AND TURNING, Naomi couldn't shut her mind off. Ghosts, ghosts, and more ghosts—they filled her mind every time she closed her eyes. She had even thought she heard a creaking sound just a few feet from her bed. Bryce was on the couch, leaving the two beds for herself and Holly. She longed to hold him right now, wishing he could drive the persistent spirits from her head. At least Genna's face hadn't appeared in her mind so far during the trip. That much was a blessing. Although no images of Bryce's ex flashed in her head, Genna wasn't far from her thoughts. *Come on. This trip is about relaxing, forgetting for the time being.*

Okay. This is easy. Just close your eyes. It's that simple. Her plan had nearly worked. Sleep was close. So close, she felt the deep release, just moments away. But then she sensed something, that prickly feeling you get when you just know that someone is watching you. Instantly, she was awake, on high alert. Her eyelids popped open but nothing was there. *See that? It's your imagination, that's all.* Closing her eyes, Naomi chuckled softly, thinking how funny this would seem in the light of the morning when she told Bryce what a chicken she was.

Seconds after she had convinced herself that her mind was working on overdrive, she felt the brush of frigid fingertips sweeping lightly across her cheek as the air chilled before her. If she kept her eyes closed, whoever or *whatever* the presence was would go away. At least that's what she had hoped.

Powerless to do anything but open her eyes and face the unknown, she gasped. Sitting before her was an unearthly woman—the same one from the upstairs window. She was sure of it. Instead of experiencing fear or dread, she felt a strange sense of peace, almost warmth. This woman, this ghost from the highest window at the B&B, wasn't here to harm her.

"You're in danger." A lone tear slid down the angelic woman's cheek. Naomi opened her mouth to speak, to reach for her, but as quickly as she had appeared, she diminished. The fading form receded, taking the cool air with it to that distant, empty place where ghosts hide in the dark shadows.

You're in danger. Naomi sat up, her heart racing from the surreal events that had just transpired. She couldn't sleep, not now. Grabbing her laptop, she walked quietly to the door, taking a peek at Bryce's sleeping form. Holly was hugging her pillow, lost in slumber. Her heartbeat slowed slightly; her loved ones were safe and thankfully oblivious to the recent paranormal events.

What else could she do when her mind raced with apprehension from the message of a beautiful spirit? Until morning came, she was powerless to act on a plan. But now? Now she could take this renewed energy and put it to work. Jules would get her book and if Naomi had her way, she would have it by the morning light.

CHAPTER EIGHTEEN

Bryce

WAKING AS THE first fingers of light drifted into the room, his eyes immediately searched for Holly and Naomi. Holly's eyes were closed, a small grin playing on her mouth. Naomi, however, was not in her bed. Glancing at the bathroom door several feet away, Bryce frowned. It didn't appear that she was in the room.

Rising to his feet, Bryce worked out the kinks in his back as he considered where she could have gone. Holly yawned and stretched out, calling for her dad.

"Hi, sweetie. Did you sleep well?" He walked over and sat beside her. Placing a quick kiss on her forehead, he wondered if Naomi was grabbing a coffee or something. That would make sense—Naomi and her coffee.

"Where's Nomi?"

"Oh, she's probably out exploring, that's all."

"But she said I could explore with her," Holly said, pouting.

"Come on. How about we get you up and ready and then we'll head out to find her."

"Fine." Holly crossed her arms, mumbling as she ambled to the bathroom.

Bryce took a moment to open the curtains and peer outside at the rumbling ocean and beach beyond. Where was Naomi and what was she up to? She should be by his side, enjoying the beautiful view.

Once he and Holly were dressed and ready to go, they made their way to the lobby. The blonde woman wasn't behind the counter this morning. Instead, a man stood, shuffling some papers.

"Good morning. Hope you're enjoying your stay."

Bryce walked over to shake the man's hand. "Yes, you have a beautiful place here. I'm Bryce and this is my daughter, Holly."

"Nice to meet you. I'm Jackson. My wife and I own Jane's Ending."

From the way Jackson straightened his shoulders when he mentioned owning this place, Bryce could sense the pride he felt. He could certainly understand that.

"Hey, by any chance did you see a brunette woman?"

Jackson smiled, pointing toward the sitting room. "Looks like she pulled an all-nighter."

Bryce held out a hand for Holly. "Thank you. It was nice to meet you, Jackson."

And there Naomi was, sound asleep with her laptop resting precariously on her thigh. He could have laughed right there except he felt something was up. It wasn't like Naomi to get up and leave in the middle of the night. Then again, how much did he even know about her nightly habits? The more he considered it, he could see Naomi getting up at all hours with a pot of coffee by her side.

"Why is she sleeping out here? Did she need a rest from exploring?" Holly wrinkled her nose, taking in Naomi's disheveled form.

"Yes, I suppose she did." Bryce approached Naomi, whose mouth was slightly ajar.

"Um, Naomi. Honey, wake up." Touching her shoulder lightly, Bryce watched as Naomi opened her eyes and adjusted to her surroundings.

"Wow. I'm sorry." Naomi rubbed her eyes. "I must have dozed off."

"You could say that. Are you okay?" Bryce sat down on a chair across from Naomi. She nodded her head in response.

"What do you say we grab some breakfast?" Bryce wasn't entirely convinced that she was being honest with him, but now wasn't the time to get into it.

"Sure, yeah. Let me get changed. Give me a few minutes?"

"Take your time."

Waiting for Naomi to get herself together, Bryce and Holly roamed around the lobby, looking at some old photographs. There was a particular photo that caught his attention. It was a faded black and white photo of a woman so breathtaking he couldn't pry his eyes from the image.

"She's a beauty, that's for sure."

"You startled me." Bryce hadn't heard Jackson approach from behind.

"Sorry about that. I can't pass by this old photo without glancing at her. That's Emily. Emily Summers. This place was hers." Jackson's eyes glazed over for a brief moment. "I guess you could say it still is."

"Come again?" His eyes darted toward Jackson.

"I just mean that Emily had so much to do with the history of the house, it's impossible to imagine this place without her."

"You said she owned it?"

Jackson scratched his face. "Something like that. Actually, there was a time when she despised this place. You see, her one-time boyfriend built this place as a boarding house for troubled young women who needed a warm bed and food in their stomachs."

"Go on." Even Holly's attention was captured by this story. Perhaps it was the way Jackson told it, with a hitch of emotion in his voice.

"Ends up her boyfriend was married and was keeping her here, out of view from his wife. He called this place Millie's—a nickname for Emily. Let's just say it didn't end well for Emily." Jackson lowered his tone at the mention of the man's marital state before stopping short, glancing down at Holly.

"Holly, honey? Do me a favor? Can you give Jackson and me a moment? Here, you can go on that app you like so much." He handed Holly his cell phone and walked her to the sitting area where she was still in sight.

Jackson stood by the picture, gazing at Emily's face. He continued to tell the rest of her story, his voice hushed. A fleeting thought popped into Bryce's head. This Jackson guy seemed to know an awful lot about the history of old Emily.

"Emily had no clue she was dating a married man. She was pretty innocent as far as experience with men went."

There he went again, it was as if Jackson had known her personally. "Excuse me, but if you don't mind me asking, how do you know so much about this Emily woman?"

Bryce followed Jackson's gaze from the lobby to the winding staircase. After a moment, he gazed at Bryce, eyes bright. "I've dedicated a lot of time and energy into learning everything I possibly can about this house."

"Oh, I see." A swift chill crept over his body, giving him instant goose bumps. Holly was sitting on the couch, chatting quietly to herself. "So what happened?"

"She—there was a fire. This place was rebuilt, from top to bottom."

He knew the answer before he even opened his mouth to speak. "And Emily?"

"She was thought to have perished from the fire, but in reality, she was shot and killed by her boyfriend's wife."

Bryce gulped. "Here?" He glanced around, feeling that familiar chill once more.

"Upstairs, in what used to be the original grand ballroom. Kind of a sad twist of fate that poor Emily was never even physical with the man and that she ended it as soon as she discovered the louse had been married." Jackson hung his head and a thick silence ensued.

"I'm sorry to hear that. That story is awful. What a beautiful woman she was, too." Naomi's words about local hauntings came back to him as he felt his pulse quicken.

"Look, I'm sorry. I don't know what came over me. Honestly, I don't make it a habit to try to scare the guests away." Jackson's halfhearted laugh didn't resonate.

Bryce's laughter sounded hollow, even to his own ears. "It's fine. No worries. It was nice to meet you." He extended his hand toward Jackson.

Bryce couldn't bring himself to look at Emily's photograph as he walked over toward Holly. Before he could give the eerie tale much more thought, he saw Naomi approaching, her eyes still shadowed.

"Ready. Let's eat."

With both of his girls nearby, Bryce shifted any unwelcome thoughts from his head. Now was the time to spend enjoying being with Naomi and Holly. This little getaway would be free of negativity, even if it killed him.

"Come on, Holly." His daughter came closer, as he heard the sound of an incoming call. Holly glanced at the phone she had been clutching.

"Phone, Daddy!" She held her tiny arm up high in the air, just close enough that he could see the caller ID.

Unfortunately Naomi's eyes also drifted to his phone at that precise moment. So much for a peaceful morning. Naomi's gaze dropped to the floor as his gut twisted.

CHAPTER NINETEEN

Naomi

IT WAS BAD enough that Genna had to call, but what was more disheartening was the way Bryce's mood flipped. As Holly chattered about any topic that took hold of her mind, Bryce nodded, responding with minimum effort. Had Holly not been sitting beside her, Naomi would have pressed Bryce as to why he was so sullen.

"What are you guys planning to do today?" Naomi kept her eyes on Bryce as she sipped her coffee.

"'You guys?' What's that all about? Didn't you say you had submitted all final touches to Jules overnight?"

Avoiding his gaze, Naomi focused on the grey ocean in the distance. "I just remembered that I forgot a few quick things. I only need a hour, two tops, and then I'm all yours."

Hesitating for a second, Bryce clenched his jaw. "Okay. Whatever you need. Holly and I will check out the pedestrian mall and then we'll swing back to the inn to pick you up. I figured we could take a drive, maybe go to the end of the Cape to the shops on the beach.

"Sure, yes. That sounds nice, Bryce."

"I want you to come to the mall too, Nomi."

"Sweetheart, I wish I could, but I'll see you soon."

Tiny arms swept out dramatically as Holly set her jaw and crossed her arms against her chest. "This is supposed to be Mommy and Daddy time." *Mommy and Daddy.* The three little words evoked such emotion.

Oh, no. On top of everything else going on, now she had disappointed Holly. It was only an hour or so, she would just have to understand.

"Listen, Holly. I'm sorry. I was supposed to work all day today, remember? But because I was able to finish last night, all I need is a little more time."

"But you said before—"

"Now, Holly. Don't give Naomi a hard time. You heard what she said, she just needs an hour or so."

"That's not right! Mommies aren't supposed to lie!"

How had the situation escalated to this? Part of Naomi felt guilty that she had let Holly down, but she had business to attend to. Important business. Feeling overly emotional, her eyes misted over and she turned her head toward the window.

"Honey, she didn't lie," Bryce began, his face a fresh shade of pink.

"She did—she did! Now she's going to leave me, just like Mommy."

Sucking in her breath, Naomi placed a shaking hand over her chest. The poor thing was traumatized by the absence of her mother. Again, she wondered, if indeed Genna had changed, would Holly be better off with her family intact?

"I, I wouldn't leave you, Holly. Ever." But hadn't she just moments ago considered doing just that? Not in the same way, of course, but heck, if Genna came back around, there would be no room for Naomi in their lives.

"Stop it. Stop it right now." Bryce's words weren't directed at his daughter, but at Naomi herself. He knew what she was thinking.

The timing couldn't have been worse, or maybe better, Naomi considered, as the waitress took that moment to approach the table, a cautious smile frozen to her face. It was the distraction they all needed.

Thank you. Naomi locked eyes with the older woman and silently expressed her gratitude.

"Check please," Bryce said.

Holly had finished her breakfast, but neither Bryce nor Naomi had taken more than a few bites since they had arrived at the small coastal diner. Silently counting to ten, Naomi winced as she looked at the pain in Bryce's eyes. This weekend getaway was supposed to make things better between them. She needed to gain control and fast.

"Holly, Bryce. Like I was saying, I need some time, an hour or two tops, and then I'm all yours." She withheld the words *I promise,* because she didn't want to break Holly's heart if something came up and she required some more time.

"Sure. Sure." Bryce shook his head to the side and then a forced smile came across his face.

"Fine." Holly's eyes met hers and she knew they would be okay. Naomi ruffled the little girl's hair and drew her in for a hug. "Love you guys, don't ever forget that."

Nodding at her, Bryce's grin changed and warmth returned to his eyes. "Let's get you back so that we can have you to ourselves."

As soon as the waitress returned and they settled up the bill, Naomi knew that the recent tension had passed, at least temporarily, and she also knew exactly who she needed to speak with.

NOW THAT BRYCE and Holly had ventured off to see the seaside shops, Naomi was determined to find out some fast facts. One thing that bothered her was that she hadn't had a chance to tell Bryce what had occurred the night before. There wasn't a moment where she had been able to grab him alone so far, so until Holly decided to go to sleep for the evening, Naomi would have to go it alone. Besides, Bryce would only worry and blame himself for bringing her to an inn that housed a resident spirit.

"Hi, good morning. I'm sorry, I forget your name." Never great with names, Naomi prided herself on recalling people's faces with great ease.

"Oh, don't be silly. I'm Kristen and heck, I usually have to meet someone at least two or three times before the name sticks." Kristen scrutinized her, squinting her eyes playfully. "Ruth?"

"Ha! Ruth? No, I'm Naomi." Knowing full well that the delightful Kristen was only trying to make her feel comfortable, she couldn't contain her laughter.

Something told her that given the right circumstances, she and Kristen could be good friends. "Okay, Kristen. I have something to ask you and please promise me you'll hear me out."

Kristen moved forward, leaning in. "Of course."

"I saw someone last night."

Turning her head slightly at Naomi's words, Kristen spoke. "I'm sorry?"

"In my room, in the middle of the night. She was by my side."

Waiting out Kristen's pause, Naomi's heart sped up. She *knew* it. Naomi had figured correctly. Kristen here might be as good an actress as they came, but Naomi detected the slight twitch in her eye and was certain that she was hiding something.

"That's impossible. I assure you nobody would be snooping around your room. Why, we only have two

other people registered right now and they're men."
Kristen took a step back. "Now if you'll excuse me."

"No." Naomi hadn't meant to grab hold of Kristen's
wrist. "I'm sorry." Removing her hand, Naomi composed
herself.

'I'm sure of it. Please, tell me who she is. I know that
you believe me because you've seen her too. It was that
woman from upstairs, when we checked in."

Releasing a pent-up sigh, Kristen ran her hands
through her smooth blonde hair. "Damn."

She barely contained her grin. "I knew it."

"Do you have time for a cup of coffee?" Kristen's
strained eyes met hers.

"Sure. Want me to grab some for both of us?"
Naomi nodded in the direction of the lobby where a
fresh pot sat waiting.

"If you wouldn't mind. I'll grab you a chair."

ONE THING NAOMI knew for sure was that it had
been longer than an hour. Mesmerized by Kristen's tale
of the breathtakingly beautiful Emily Summers, she could
only exhale and try to piece together all she had learned.

"What I don't understand is why she's back. Like I
mentioned, once Jackson freed her soul from centuries of
loneliness and agony, we never felt her presence again.
Why now, why you?"

An unmistakable chill forced its way through Naomi and she shuddered, wondering precisely the same thing.

"And the warning?" Kristen's eyes clouded over to a stormier shade of blue. "Tell me about yourself. Don't leave anything out."

Skipping right to the punch, Naomi delivered. "I'm a writer and I'm being pursued by the evil spirit of my ex-boyfriend." She closed her eyes, not welcoming the expected expression. Instead of seeing fear, ridicule, or disbelief, Naomi only saw recognition and understanding.

"Go on." Kristen prompted her to continue.

When Naomi finally finished explaining the mess she was involved in, she shielded herself against Kristen's reaction.

"A writer, huh?"

Of all the details Naomi had just thrown out there, the fact that she was an author was the one that caught Kristen's attention? "Why, yes."

"I forgot to mention that I, or rather, my husband and I, jointly wrote the story of Emily. We had it published."

Now that was a book Naomi needed to read. "Wow, that's incredible. I hope it's going well."

"That's neither here nor there, but thanks. Our goal was to get Emily's story out there, her *real* story, as part of the healing process for her. We wanted her to have peace."

And now Naomi had somehow stirred the spirit's emotions, called to her on some level. She wouldn't deny that she felt some guilt at disrupting Emily, however unintentional it had been on her part. There she went again, disturbing these ghosts. Or perhaps they were disturbing her, now that she considered it.

"I'm sorry if by my being here, I have upset her and you."

"Please! Emily is a grown woman. Believe me when I tell you she can stand on her own two feet. She's the most courageous person I know. I'm sure of one thing: if she's here after all this time—which by the way, I think she is—she's got a purpose."

"Which is?" Naomi pressed Kristen.

"It sounds like she's here to warn you, to help protect you to the best of her ability." Kristen bobbed her head up and down. "Problem is, I don't know exactly how much she can do and how much time she has."

"What do you mean?"

"I don't know much other than that as far as the spirit world goes, how much do we really know?"

It was true. Maggie had experienced great difficulty communicating with her, Ryan was plain perplexed, and Nick? Oh, Nick. An unwelcome shudder returned.

"Wait a minute." Kristen lifted her gaze and hope grazed her soft features. "Why, that's it."

"What? What's it?'

"It's perfect. Listen, Jackson's cousin has a friend. She's a bit eccentric, but hey, it's worth a shot."

"What are you thinking?"

"She's a medium—a channeler, to be exact. Not only does she have the ability to communicate by inner seeing, but she can also allow the spirit to merge with her aura. In other words, she's pretty tuned into otherworldly beings. The way I figure it, if she is as good as some claim she is, then she just might be able to direct you on the right path."

"That's amazing. You say she's got a decent reputation?"

"Does the fact that her waiting list for appointments is over a year tell you anything? Heck, I wish I had known about her when we were dealing with Emily and all of her turmoil a few years back."

"I'm afraid I don't have a year. I can't continue like this." Thoughts of her recent strained relationship with Bryce haunted her. Genna's latest attempt to call him was still fresh in her thoughts, baiting her to fall down that dark hole once more.

"I have a connection, let's see if we can get you in. I'm not promising a miracle here, just some help."

"That would be incredible. If it's one thing I'm open to, it's help."

Kristen raised a manicured finger, signaling for Naomi to hold on. She grabbed her cell and started making calls.

While Kristen was doing that, Naomi's eye wandered to the framed black and white photograph hanging on the wall nearby. Sucking in her breath, she took in the ethereal beauty of Emily Summers. Stunning didn't quite describe Emily's aura. There was more to her, Naomi sensed it by the faint touch the spirit had placed upon her cheek last night.

"It helps to have friends in the right places."

"Excuse me?" Emily's spell was broken by Kristen's comment.

"You're in. Just so happens that Lydia can see you in about two hours." Kristen smiled at her. Two hours. That was amazing, but she had promised Holly and Bryce that she would be all theirs in an hour or so.

"Did you hear what I said?"

Shaking her head, Naomi swallowed back her troubled thoughts. "I—yes. Thank you so much, I really appreciate your help."

Kristen came from around the small counter. "No worries. You can use all the help you can get. I know that because I've been there." Kristen spun to face Emily's portrait. "As much as I admire that magnificent woman, there was a time not so long ago when she scared the crap out of me."

Her own gaze drifted to the photograph. 'Hard to believe she could have been a menacing presence around here."

"Hell, she certainly was. Emily, if you can hear me now, I apologize for saying that, but let's remember how much you despised me at first."

Kristen had explained earlier that Emily had been quite jealous of Kristen's relationship with Jackson at the time, so much so that Emily had caused her to fall down the spiral staircase, among other things.

"Not that I don't love you. You know I do." Kristen's tone faded to a whisper as she addressed the woman in the antique photo.

It was like how Naomi felt about Maggie. Naomi could relate to that kind of fondness, that level of love that could form. She and Maggie had shared such a strong, impenetrable bond.

"Do you have the directions?"

"Sure do, but I can do even better than that if you wish. The other two guests checked out and Jackson is around. I could drive you over, it's not far."

How did Naomi luck out in finding this generous person? "I'd like that."

CHAPTER TWENTY

Naomi

BRYCE HAD TAKEN Holly to a park with a playground and Naomi finally had the opportunity to call him and explain things with Holly out of hearing distance.

Bryce wasn't pleased, but after she had taken the time to share why she had spent the previous evening in the lobby of the inn, he seemed to understand.

"Be safe."

"Of course. Listen, I feel awful about this, about everything. I have a lot of making up to do with both you and that beautiful daughter of yours."

"Nonsense. I'm lucky to have you in my life. You just concentrate on getting rid of Nick and staying out of harm's way."

His words reminded Naomi of all the reasons she loved him so much. "Have fun. I'll tell you everything tonight after Holly goes to bed. I love you, Bryce."

"I love you, too."

After she had disconnected her call, Naomi stared at her cell for a moment. She cherished Bryce and Holly so much, but felt threatened by Nick's and Genna's menacing presence in their lives. It was as if the two of them had gotten together and conferred with one another about the best ways to make her life miserable.

Count your blessings. Her mother's sensible mantra crossed her mind as Naomi did just that. She had Bryce, Holly, Amy, and Miriam to call her loved ones. Something told her that she would soon be adding Kristen to her list.

"Everything okay?"

"Huh? Oh, sure. I guess I have a lot on my mind."

Kristen glanced at her and then returned her gaze to the road ahead of them. "Trouble with that handsome guy of yours?"

"I don't necessarily know that I'd call it *trouble,* but between the both of us, we have a lot on our plate right now."

"That stinks. I'm a good listener if you feel like talking."

Of course she was. Kristen seemed to be skilled in anything she put her mind to. "Ah, his ex-wife is back in the picture. Get this: she disappears, leaving her little girl

159

and Bryce. Now, over a year later, she returns and wants them back."

Silence filled the air for the briefest of moments. When Kristen turned to her, her eyes held such empathy. "I'm sorry. That's a tough one."

"I know." There she went again, questioning herself, wondering if there was the slightest chance that Holly would be happier with her parents back together. Knowing Bryce, because of the fact that he had made a promise to Naomi, she knew he wouldn't backtrack. He would never disappoint her, but if they were both better off with Genna, wasn't it up to Naomi to give up the one person she loved most in this world?

"What are you thinking?"

Naomi managed to expel a bitter laugh. "Trust me, you don't want to know."

"Then if you're thinking that they would be better off with the little girl's mom in the picture, I'm going to tell you something."

She captured Naomi's interest. Nodding her head at Kristen, she listened intently.

"I see the way he looks at you. I noticed it when you first came in. And his daughter? It's the same with her. They love you. You're their world, I'm sure of it."

"Thank you." There was some relief in Kristen's words.

"I mean it. And this ex of his? She can't be wrapped too tightly if she disappears without a trace, leaving those two behind. How could she possibly be a good influence on her daughter?"

"You're right. God, you're so right, but people can change, can't they?"

"In my opinion, not that much. I might be wrong here, but my gut tells me I'm spot on and my gut is rarely wrong."

Placing a warm hand over hers, Kristen drove to their destination. Sometimes it took another woman to gain perspective. Naomi was thankful she had met her.

ONCE THEY HAD arrived at Lydia's house, Naomi peered around the property noting that the house appeared neat and tidy. It all seemed so normal, except she needed to remind herself that her reason for being here was the furthest thing from customary.

An elderly brunette answered the door, her arms guiding them inside. "Nice to see you again, Kristen. It's been a long time."

"Yes. And thanks for seeing Naomi here on such short notice."

"Yes, thank you. I can't tell you how much I appreciate it."

Lydia grinned at Naomi, but then turned her attention back to Kristen. She grabbed hold of Kristen's hands and practically beamed. "Is there something you'd like to share with me?"

Kristen flushed a deep pink; her eyes darted from Lydia to Naomi and finally rested on Lydia once more. "You are good."

What were they talking about? Naomi felt lost in the conversation. Watching Kristen's smile grow, she began to piece everything together.

"Are you—"

"Yes. I'm pregnant."

She barely knew this woman, but found herself wrapping her arms around Kristen, gushing about the baby news. "This is amazing." How did Lydia figure it out? It wasn't as if Kristen were even showing in the slightest.

"I told you she was the best." Kristen winked at Lydia and then dismissed herself as she headed for the living room.

"Come, my office is straight ahead, second door to the right."

From all outward appearances, there was nothing eccentric about Lydia. Not knowing what to expect, Naomi realized what she hadn't anticipated was a standard office, and Lydia's space was just that.

"I don't want you to say a word, not a word about your purpose for being here. It always works best when one is a clean slate, if you will."

Lydia directed Naomi to a small love seat and dimmed the lighting, allowing the room to become a bit more conducive to relaxing.

"I'm going to say some things to you– some of which may or may not make sense at the time. Please follow along and tell me as we proceed if you can relate to what I'm saying."

Nodding in agreement, Naomi swallowed and prepared herself.

Lydia said a small blessing to those spirits, living and dead, that would be present in the room. The medium reached for her hands, squeezing slightly before releasing her. Opening her mouth to speak, Naomi watched as Lydia's eyes shut tightly. She closed her mouth, holding back her question. It seemed Lydia didn't require much of her other than her presence in this room.

"I don't know, I don't like this." Lydia's eyes remained closed as she shook her head from side to side.

Eager to understand what Lydia was mumbling about, she leaned forward, scrunching her brows as her pulse quickened. What was it?

Abruptly, Lydia sat back as her eyes flew open. Her lids fluttered as she fought to steady her quaking hands. "Naomi—"

"What is it? What did you see?" Something was off here, she could see it written on Lydia's taut features.

"He, they, whatever this entity is that's trying to consume you, attempted to overpower me. It doesn't work that way, I don't operate like that."

"I'm sorry, but I don't understand what you're saying."

"I'm a channeler. I practice conscious channeling. What I'm saying is that I'm always in control. I can stop the spirit from taking over my body any time I choose. This, this entity or entities that are surrounding you, they're strong, overpowering."

"*They?* Why do you say *they?* It's one spirit only, his name is Nick."

Shaking her head forcefully, Lydia was quick to disagree. "No. You're wrong. He's got help and quite honestly, I'm terrified to go back to them."

"That's it? I need you, I need help. If you can't help me, then what am I supposed to do?" Helplessness was not a welcome feeling. Lydia couldn't let her down.

"I don't know, Naomi. I want to help you, I really do—"

"Then help me. I'm begging you." She grabbed hold of Lydia's hands, pressing down hard. It happened so quickly, she could have blinked and missed it. Watching Lydia's eyes glaze over, Naomi gasped.

Mere seconds passed before Lydia jerked forward in her chair. Opening her eyes, the woman before her smirked and squinted directly at her. A chill swept through the room and her body. Shivering, Naomi wrapped her arms around herself, standing up. She backed up toward the far wall as Lydia approached stealthily.

"He's better off without you. A child needs her mother. I'll make your life a living hell, just like you did to me. I'll gladly return the favor."

Lydia was rambling, her voice ranging from a deep, husky tone to a higher pitched, smoother one. Back and forth, high and low. "I'm in no rush, I can play with you for years if I need to, before it's over. You led him to me, it's all your fault, all your fault, all your fault!"

Lydia's eyes popped wide, her veins bulging as she reached for Naomi. No, not here. Nick's reach couldn't extend this far. She was the fool who had encouraged this, asked Lydia to expose herself to him. Blood pounding through her ears, seeing red, Naomi clenched her fists hard, ready to fight.

"Stop it, Nick! Stop!"

Lydia gained space between them and took hold of Naomi's hair, pulling with a strength that a woman her age couldn't possibly own. Shaking, shaking and pounding. A strong but slender hand clutched her throat, squeezing. Fighting for breath and life, Naomi pushed, her arms on fire. Tears streamed down her face as Naomi's world went from gray to black.

CHAPTER TWENTY-ONE

Bryce

SHE WASN'T LETTING up. Couple the fact that Genna was relentlessly calling him with the concern that Naomi wasn't responding to his attempts to reach her, Bryce felt as if he was slowly losing his grip.

It had been at least two hours since he had last spoken with Naomi. Sensing that something was wrong, he was helpless to a solution. He should have insisted that Naomi tell him the name and address of the medium. But wait—Naomi had mentioned that Kristen from the inn was driving her. Surely Kristen's husband would know where this medium lived.

"Holly, come on. Let's take a walk to the lobby."

Luckily Holly had been so distracted by the playground and then a trip to get an ice cream cone that she hadn't questioned Naomi's whereabouts.

"Okay, Daddy. Let me get Tiger." Holly grabbed her stuffed leopard and took her father's hand as they headed out the door and down the hallway. Before he was even able to approach the front desk, Bryce saw them from a distance. His stomach dropped when Naomi's gaze met his. The stretched neckline of her shirt gave way to red splotches covering the base of her neck.

As if on autopilot, Bryce sprinted to her and squeezed her close. She sobbed openly, clinging to him as Kristen took a step back, allowing the couple to have some space. Jackson stepped out from behind the counter in a flash.

"What the hell happened to her?" Bryce finally looked toward Kristen, his eyes pleading for answers while Holly pulled on Bryce's jacket. How could he have forgotten that Holly had just witnessed his panic?

"Holly, it's okay. I'm fine. I just tripped and fell at the store. I'll be fine, sweetie."

Leave it to Naomi to think about Holly when she was down. "Yes, she's going to be okay. Kristen, Jackson? Can you please show Holly around the inn? She's been after me to take a tour. Now would be the perfect time."

"You're okay?" Holly's eyes scrutinized Naomi.

"Yup. Now go ahead and learn everything you can about this amazing place." Naomi leaned over, flinching slightly before placing a soft kiss atop Holly's head.

Thankful that he could trust Kristen and Jackson with his daughter for a few minutes, Bryce's attention focused on Naomi. "Are you okay?" He pulled sections of her hair from her scalp as she flinched.

"I will be once this is all over."

"Do you need to go to the hospital?"

"No, I promise you I'm just banged up a little, but we need to talk. This medium, Lydia, she saw it all. Bryce, he's growing stronger. He took over her body, that's never happened to her before. She told me she's never lost control." Naomi's lip quivered.

"Oh, Naomi. What happened? How did he do this to you?"

"Through Lydia. She's pretty shaken up. And it's worse. Lydia swears there's two of them; spirits, that is."

"Two? But who else?"

"I don't know and I don't have the strength to even speculate right now. But he, they, whoever was there, they spoke in quick, choppy sentences. Bryce, they said you and Holly should be with Genna."

As terrible as the news was, Bryce felt a wave of relief wash over him. He felt so light that he actually grabbed her. "Do you realize what that means?"

Holding her head in her hands, Naomi sighed deeply. "My head is throbbing, I have no idea."

"I suspected this before, but now after hearing what you just said, I'm sure of it. It's psychological warfare, don't you see what he's doing to you?'

Naomi's lifted her gaze to meet his eyes. "You're right. Damn it, Bryce. I knew it, but hadn't considered the depths he would sink."

"Of course. It all makes sense. Nick is clever if not anything else. He's hitting you below the belt, as I've suspected."

"Where it hurts most," Naomi continued. "He's trying to take away the two people that matter most in this world to me. I had suspected he may be involved with planting some of these thoughts in my head, but I was also seriously starting to question my own sanity. He's brilliant, in a sick, twisted way, of course. What better way to tear us apart than to make me slowly lose my mind over Genna."

"And to have us argue."

"That night back at the restaurant. I was a sleep deprived, over-caffeinated mess. I'm sorry, Bryce."

"It's okay. Now that we have proof positive that Nick is indeed involved, you have to beat him at his own game. You're tough, Naomi, don't let him drag you down."

"I know, Bryce. I believe this Genna business is his handiwork, but I have to ask you this just one more time."

She didn't need to speak the words. "No, Naomi. I only want you. Since that first time I walked over to your house to introduce myself, I was a goner."

"But what if? What if Genna had some kind of breakdown and she's truly meant to be with you guys?'

"I have to tell you this. Even before she left, she wasn't half the woman you are. Nobody is." Gently, he parted her hair and kissed the top of her head.

"Thank you, Bryce. I really needed to hear that. I won't let the two of you down. I'd rather die first."

Standing there, holding Naomi close, Bryce had only one thing on his mind and that was taking in Naomi's fresh, clean scent, allowing his senses to get lost in her. Once they got back home, he knew that he needed to become a more active participant in fighting Nick. This was taking a toll on Naomi. She was spending too much time battling this demon on her own. He could join Naomi in her quest for peace and keep his daughter far from harm. Nick thought he was a force to reckon with? The spirit had no idea how tough and unyielding Bryce could become when defending his loved ones.

"Tomorrow, when we head back, you're no longer alone. You're going to include me in everything you say, think, plan and do when it comes to Nick."

She melted into his arms as she surrendered to him. He could actually feel her relief. "That sounds perfect."

THE REST OF the day and that evening was quiet. It was what they all needed. Even Holly was low key, as if she sensed that everyone required some down time. The trio had ventured into town for a pleasant dinner at one of the favored local restaurants. After dinner, once Holly was fast asleep, he and Naomi had shared a bottle of red wine on the tiny balcony of their room. The slight chill didn't deter them from snuggling up in the fresh air, wrapped in a cozy, oversized quilt. The consistent roar of the waves pounding in the distance soothed his nerves.

It was when they had said good night to one another and he was in that drowsy state just before sleep consumed him that he saw her. At first, he thought someone had broken into their room. Sitting up in a flash, Bryce sucked in his breath.

The glowing, tranquil light surrounding the woman clued him in that he was not dealing with a living human being. When the figure turned and exposed her fragile profile, he knew then and there it was Emily. Ever so slowly, she bent down and lay a delicate palm on top of Naomi's head, kissing the exact spot of her injury. Unable to do anything but watch, Bryce fell into a trance. Naomi had no idea that Emily was in the room, let alone touching her.

His heart ached as the graceful ghostly form turned to face him. Her glowing, impossibly green eyes practically stole his breath. She was by his side now, reaching for his hand. Allowing Emily to take hold of him, he couldn't pry his eyes from her.

"It's not what it seems."

No words would come when he opened his mouth. He wanted to ask what she had meant, but his words stuck in his throat. Her icy fingers glided up his arm and she pulled him close, and then closer still. Fear wasn't a consideration as he sank deeper into her magical spell.

Her lips closed in on his, mere centimeters from grazing his mouth. Closing his eyes, he tried to push away, even in his trance. Closer she came and this time he was actually able to resist and clear his head.

"She's safe with you, just as I had hoped." Releasing him now, she kissed her own hand and blew the frosty air in his direction. "She needs you, don't let her down."

And she was gone. What the hell had just happened? Now that Bryce's head had cleared completely, he gained some perspective. Emily had been testing him. Testing him to see if he was worthy of Naomi. Now Emily was telling him that he needed to protect her.

Leaving Naomi on her own was never an option, but now he felt even stronger about their relationship. He would have never considered that their bond could grow stronger, but this bittersweet weekend away had brought them impossibly close. Between her horrifying experience and the approval of Emily Summers, he was lost. Lost in the love of a woman he could never see himself without. It was him and Naomi, through good and bad. Together, he knew they had the ability to fight the supernatural demons who threatened to come between them and turn out even stronger in the end.

CHAPTER TWENTY-TWO

Naomi

"I STILL CAN'T figure out exactly what he wants from you. I mean, wouldn't it be easier if you could simply figure out exactly how Nick died, bring down justice to those responsible, therefore giving Nick the closure he's seeking?"

"But Miriam, don't you see? It's beginning to look as if Nick doesn't even know what he wants from me. I think his lines are becoming blurred. He's losing any ounce of sanity he may have once had. I think his sole purpose now is to get revenge on me for sending him to jail and everything that followed."

Phil and Miriam had joined her for breakfast at the diner near Miriam's place.

The first thing Naomi had done when she arrived was to apologize for her behavior from their recent dinner. Phil had accepted and now she hoped they could put the evening behind them. It had only been one night since she had returned from Cape Florence, but she had slept surprisingly well. As a result, she had only drank one cup of coffee so far this morning. If she wanted to beat Nick, she would have to keep a clear head.

"So, on my end, I've searched the prison's visitors log for anyone who may have visited Nick prior to his death."

"And? Did anyone of interest show up?" Naomi almost blurted out the doctor's name and then remembered how all the trouble at dinner had started with Phil.

"Of course Uncle Frank had visited, and there was the past visit from you." Miriam nibbled at her toast and then gently placed it down on her plate.

"That's it?"

"That's all, but . . ."

"Oh no, don't start this again." Phil placed a heavy hand on the table and sighed.

"Phil, I told you we needed to speak and I'm not going to hold anything back."

"Go on, please." Naomi needed answers and it seemed that Miriam had something of interest here.

"The prison doctor did admit to being friendly with Dr. Bender."

"So what? What does that mean? That because Dan knows the prison doctor he killed Nick? That's absurd! This is a small town and people are connected."

"Phil? Nobody is accusing Dan of doing a damn thing. You need to calm the hell down and take a breather." Miriam ran a slender hand through her smooth, blonde hair, taking a peek around her at the other customers.

"Sorry. I'm sorry. Listen, do you guys want to know my opinion as an outsider?"

Naomi summoned all the strength she had to remain neutral. Why did Miriam have to bring Phil anyway? The more Naomi got to know Phil, the less he had in common with his brother. Ryan had been sweet and considerate. Phil was proving to be a pain in her ass as far as Naomi was concerned. It was no wonder the two brothers had drifted apart before Ryan's death.

Tapping her foot, Naomi inhaled deeply, waiting for Phil to continue. For the sake of her friendship with Miriam, she wouldn't share her feelings where Phil was concerned. If he made her friend happy, what could she say? From past experience, she knew negative comments could only hurt their friendship.

"What I think is that Nick overdosed, whether deliberately or unintentionally, but that's *it*. You guys are searching for something that probably doesn't exist. Maybe he's just plain pissed at you, Naomi, and the world in general."

Biting her lip, Naomi felt heat rise in her face. Nick was the man who had caused Ryan to die, whether it was an accident or not. He was also the guy who covered up the accident and led everyone to believe poor Maggie had drowned.

"Do you understand that your brother was killed because of that monster?" Naomi leaned forward, speaking through her clenched teeth. Surprisingly enough, Miriam crossed her arms and sat back, watching the interaction between her friend and boyfriend without interjecting.

"Of course I do! Don't you think I remember that fact every single day of my life? My brother died because of him and for that I will never forgive him, but trying to pin the murder on my friend? Dan Bender holds the utmost respect of this community and if by the off chance someone did murder Nick, I would say he got what he deserved, but I'll be damned if I let you accuse a good friend whom I know is innocent."

Miriam had winced noticeably at the mention of Nick deserving to be killed and now it seemed she could no longer hold her tongue. "Phil, you should really watch your words, what with an open murder investigation going on. And nobody is accusing Dr. Bender of anything other than possibly helping to support Nick's probable addiction to painkillers."

It was Naomi's turn to sit back and watch this time. Phil's gaze bounced between Naomi and Miriam, finally settling on the front door of the diner. "With all due respect, *Officer Marty*, I've about had enough of this quaint little breakfast." Scooting back, he then pulled his chair out and stomped out of sight. Naomi watched Miriam's eyes follow him out the door.

"I'm sorry."

Waving a dismissive hand, Miriam forced a grin that Naomi knew wasn't heartfelt. "It's nothing. He'll get over it."

"Are you guys *that* friendly with Dan Bender? I mean, Phil's acting as if Dr. Bender is his best friend, for God's sake."

"We have gone out a few times as couples and they play golf together at least once a month, but I wouldn't say they're particularly close. I think Phil respects his position in this town. I also feel that by stirring up Nick's death, it's bringing back all the memories of Ryan's death. That can't be easy on him, Naomi."

Naomi took a swig of her coffee and nodded for the waitress to bring a refill. As long as she was sleeping, she could handle the caffeine. "I know it can't be. I'm not unsympathetic toward Phil, not at all."

"Maybe you can ease off him just a bit where Dr. Bender is concerned?"

"I won't say anything else around Phil if at all possible, but why did he even come to breakfast, knowing we would be discussing Nick?"

Her question gave Miriam pause, and when she spoke her words were deliberate. "Phil has been doing quite a bit of soul-searching in the area of Ryan lately. He expressed that he feels guilty for the recent distance between him and Ryan."

Naomi had often wondered why the brothers had lost their closeness and exactly how close they had ever been. Wishing she had grilled Ryan about his sibling while she had the chance, Naomi could only wonder and speculate now.

"Did Phil ever say if the two of them had a falling out? I mean, why the distance in their relationship? Did it start as a geographic problem?" Naomi considered in this day and age, communicating with a loved one across the country or even across the world was super easy.

"Not exactly, no. Just that they were two different people, and that their lifestyles weren't similar. Ryan, we know, was a free spirit, with a passion for life. Phil had moved across the country to start over after a failed relationship and a job opportunity in one of the West Coast offices of his company."

"I can agree on the fact that although they have similar appearances, their personalities couldn't differ more. Ryan wore his heart in his sleeve and yes, his passion for all things was, well, off the charts. You couldn't find a better friend than him."

"Gee, Naomi, you're certainly not painting a very positive image of my guy here." Miriam chugged her coffee and then rolled her shoulders back.

Realizing too late that Miriam was correct, she felt bad for the harsh comparison. "I honestly don't know Phil all that well, so I apologize. All I know is that you're an excellent judge of character and if you love him, then that's good enough for me. Let's just say that Ryan was

178

less confrontational—and that's not always a bad thing, to stick up for what you believe to be true." Naomi knew she was backtracking here, but she wanted things to be okay between her and Miriam, and besides, how well did she really know Phil? Who was she to judge? Naomi shifted in her seat.

"First of all, stop wiggling around, I'm cool." Miriam's gaze zeroed in on Naomi. "Can I tell you something?"

"Of course. What is it?" Leaning forward, Naomi didn't like the concern etched on her friend's face.

"I care a lot about Phil, I do—" Miriam's eyes shifted to the floor.

"But?"

"Oh, it's nothing, really. I guess what I'm trying to say is that lately, at times, he seems irrational and moody. Maybe it comes from the fact that I lived alone without a boyfriend for so long. I'm keeping an eye on it, that's all."

For Miriam to express any doubts about this guy she had been crazy about not so long ago made Naomi sad for her. Maybe she was pushing things too far. Making a mental note to back off on the subject of Phil, Naomi reached over and took hold of her friend's hands.

"What I think is that we're all under a tremendous amount of stress with this Nick business. Bryce and I were having a lot of problems as well."

"I guess, but . . ."

"We just got back from a weekend away and it did us a world of good. I know we still have many more burdens to overcome before we put Nick to rest, but it helped. Perhaps you should consider doing the same."

Nodding her head up and down, Miriam's eyes misted. "I don't have more than a day to myself for at least a month, but thank you, I'll consider it. But Naomi?"

Naomi cocked her head to the side, noticing the shadows under Miriam's eyes for the first time. "What is it?"

"How did you know? I mean really *know*, that you and Bryce were meant to be together?"

That was an easy one. "You just know. It comes from a feeling that you can't live without that person and they make your days so much brighter. When it's the real thing, you don't have to question it." Her last words faded.

"Except if you're a person like me who questions everything, right?"

A giggle escaped as Naomi squeezed Miriam's hands tightly. "You just have to relax, okay?"

"Sure, Naomi. Thank you." Miriam squeezed Naomi's hands in return.

TRUE TO HIS word, Bryce had made himself available to her since they had returned from the weekend getaway several days ago. Then again, Naomi had always known she had his full support. The difference, she supposed, was that Naomi now included Bryce in all of her thoughts and actions concerning Nick.

Nick was absent, and she made the most of the calm before the impending storm. Gaining her strength from Bryce's consistent communication and sleeping for blissful hours at a time, she felt stronger than ever. Even thoughts of Genna were diminishing.

The well-needed break from all things paranormal served to refresh her, but caught her off guard when Nick returned with a vengeance. It started with the nightmare of Bryce and Genna's second wedding. The two couldn't keep their hands off one another when they repeated their vows. Physical intimacy during the night of their wedding was tough to view up close and personal, especially considering the fact that Naomi wasn't typically a lucid dreamer. It wasn't until she woke sweating, her heart racing in her chest, that she figured out it was all an awful, albeit vivid, dream.

Before she had a chance to fully recover from the blow of Nick's nighttime torture, he appeared before her, dressed in all black, his hood drawn tightly over his graying, hollow cheekbones.

"Nick, I don't know why you're prolonging this. Why can't you just tell me what you need from me!" she called out to his approaching form. Pounding, advancing footsteps closed the walls in around her, making her bedroom into a darkening room of horror.

Nick had the advantage of swiftness, but it didn't mean she wouldn't try to escape. Edging her way to the doorway, somehow she left her bedroom behind her and raced for the stairs. Zelda's agile form pounced swiftly ahead of her.

Her fight-or-flight instinct kicked into full gear and her feet slammed down each step, speeding to the bottom of the staircase. Lungs afire, Naomi screamed for Bryce, scorching her throat even more. But there Nick was, at the very bottom step, snickering with his arms open.

"Come here, sweetheart." His menacing tone chilled her to the core, stopping her short. She had nowhere to turn, but she could fight. Now her instinct to run was surpassed by that to battle him.

Slamming into his chest, she punched out in a futile attempt to overpower Nick's increasingly overwhelming presence. Right now he allowed her to make a fool of herself as he stood still, bellowing with a sick laughter she wouldn't soon forget.

Her ragged breathing gave way to her final, weakening punch. Knowing she was done, she sank to the floor, collapsing at his feet in defeat.

"You done yet? Feel better?" He gently lowered himself to the carpet beside her. With light fingers, he parted her hair to see her face. Naomi dared to look him in the eye. For a brief second Naomi thought he would spare her whatever horrors he had in store, but his eyes glazed a dark gray and his wicked grin widened, his foul breath hot on her face.

"Let's play." Before she could attempt to resist him, he grabbed her sore head and pulled her close, wrapping his long arms around her body, suffocating her as she choked, fighting for breath. In the distance, she thought she heard Bryce's voice screaming out for her, but it was probably her imagination, holding out for a last shred of hope. Passing out cold, Naomi lost her grip on reality.

Not sure how much time had passed, Naomi awoke, every nerve in her body quaking with sheer terror. She lay in the cold wet earth, sucking in her breath as she fought the bitter stench and enveloping darkness. Smashing at the wall above her, bits of dirt tumbled down. Screaming, she opened her mouth wider to call out as dank soil crumbled into her mouth. Gasping through her tears, Naomi knew she couldn't give up. Her fight was all she had. Determined to block out her surroundings, she strengthened her grip on the earth above her and pushed out.

Over and over she fought, holding back her warm tears now as a fresh sense of determination took hold. Bryce—he was waiting for her and she was coming back for him and the little girl who meant the world to her.

Shoving her arms up, she screeched out as she tore at the soil with her fingertips, large chunks of fresh dirt breaking through. Gasping short, quick breaths, she struggled to rise out of the cold trench she had been placed into.

Moonlight lit her way out of the hole as she took in her surroundings. Wiping mud and soil from her face, she swallowed the grit already in her mouth. What did Nick think he was doing to her and where the hell was that monster?

Stomping through the darkness, Naomi froze when she recognized her surroundings. She shouldn't have been surprised to see her own home before her, stretched out in the distance of the desolate night. She should have felt relief, but instead her stomach dropped and wet tears streamed down her face and neck, turning an icy cold.

It was too dark. That was the first sign something was amiss. Dark and empty. Picking up speed, Naomi then glanced down at her shoes, not noticing before they were her highest pair of heels, not to mention the most uncomfortable.

Bastard. Naomi reached down to take off her shoes, feeling cold in her bones. It didn't help that she was still in her short, flimsy nightgown. Nick didn't spare the tiniest details.

Glancing down at her muddy gown, she then focused her attention, holding her head high and purposeful. She was almost there, not quite upon her house when she saw the sign as she came around the driveway.

For Sale.

What was this about? If it was part of a twisted, Nick-induced dream, she was lucid enough to realize this was not her reality. Which meant that it most likely was not, in fact, a dream. Shaking hands reached out to open her front door. Her eyes widened as she twisted and turned, her jagged fingernails smearing traces of blood on the doorknob. What was this? She pounced to the window with bare, raw feet and strained to see inside. From out here in the cold night air, all she could make out was darkness. Where was Zelda? Where was Bryce?

Bryce.

Turning her head, she spied his lit house just up the path from her home. Sprinting, she ignored the pain of small rocks and cold gravel on the soles of her already tender feet. "Bryce! Bryce!" She picked up speed, her lungs sucked in the chilly night air.

Standing at Bryce's front door, she reached her hand out to open the door, but stopped. Her gut told her not to enter the home of this man whom she loved so much. Instead, she turned to peek through the living room window and bellowed at the sight before her as her blood-stained fingers pressed on the glass.

It could have been a photograph from a magazine about warm, inviting homes. The fireplace roared, displaying enough light for Naomi to see every minute detail of the scene playing out before her. Bryce, Holly, and Genna sat on the couch. Bryce wrapped his arms around Genna as she sat reading a book with Holly pressed close against her. Holly gazed up adoringly at her mother as Naomi stopped breathing.

This is not real. This is not real. Naomi repeated the phrase over and over again until she had no idea how long she had been standing there watching what appeared to be the perfect family reunion.

Had she died? Was her body, in fact, in that cold, shallow ditch? She spun to glance toward the realtor sign and sank to her knees, weeping openly.

So this is what had happened to Bryce's life *if* or *when* she had died? He went *back* to Genna? How could he? How could he have done this? How could she have allowed it to happen? *What have I done? What can I do?*

If this was her reality, she was cursed. Screwed in the worst possible way. Curling her dirt-smeared arms around her quaking body, Naomi lay under Bryce's window sobbing until everything around her ceased to exist. In the end it was to be her, just Naomi, left to face her fate alone.

CHAPTER TWENTY-THREE

Naomi

NAOMI AWOKE WITH a slight nudge. Opening her eyes, she gasped as she looked around Bryce's yard. Who had touched her? Spinning her head from one direction to the other, she couldn't locate a single soul.

Relief washed over Naomi as she realized she might still have some chance, some hope in this otherwise bleak situation.

Although still dark, the first hints of a promised dawn filled the air. Crashing visions of being trapped in the earth, of Bryce and Genna, consumed her. Her gaze dropped to her flimsy white gown. A squeaky clean, pure white gown adorned her. Next to her, the ridiculously high heels from a party years earlier, lay beside her.

What is happening to me? Stumbling to her feet, Naomi knew two things. One, she was cold, and two, she needed to find her way home, if that was even an option. A renewed sense of purpose swept over her. She held her head high, ignoring Bryce's glaring front bay window. She didn't want to see Bryce and Genna again, wouldn't torture herself with Genna coming back to Bryce and Holly.

As she walked toward her house, her eyes scanned for that sickening realtor sign in her yard and sure enough, it was there, like a glaring beacon. Her stomach dropped. Where was she to go?

Forward or backward?

Glancing back at Bryce's house, she thought she detected the slightest sound.

Naomi. Naomi.

There it was again. This time, she focused all of her energy on it; she could now make out the voice and knew who it was that was calling for her.

Bryce.

Bryce. He needed her.

She needed him.

Naomi didn't give a crap if Genna was there playing the role of the happy housewife because she and Bryce belonged together. She heard the pain in his voice when he had called to her from beyond.

I'm coming to you, Bryce. Hold on, I'm almost there.

Slinging her shoes upward, she slowly made her way to his house, silent and steady, with purpose and determination. Something or someone gave her the fortitude she so desperately needed to reach Bryce's front door. Even her hands were unshakeable as she opened the front door and advanced into the living room, despite the sound of Genna's high-pitched laughter.

"Get out." At first, Naomi's fragile voice betrayed her, but then she heard Bryce once more, his tone firmer, more insistent.

"Get out! Get out! Get out!" Naomi drew closer to Genna and Bryce. Holly must have been upstairs, which was a blessing.

Upon hearing the other woman cackle, she clenched her slender fists.

"Who do you think you are? He chose *me*. He wants *me*." Genna's eyes challenged her, glowing with deception.

At that precise moment, she saw the cold, hard truth. It couldn't have been clearer.

Naomi's mind fit all the pieces together. Why hadn't she pieced it together before? Her hands reached out, as if they had a mind of their own.

"Naomi! What are you doing here? You can't be— you're dead." Bryce's eyes glazed as his jaw dropped.

This isn't real. This isn't happening.

Genna's eyes mocked her, taunting her to take action.

Come home to me, Naomi. I can't do this without you. Bryce's words from beyond gave her all the power she needed to finish this, to set things right.

Although in this universe a perplexed Bryce stood rooted to the spot, in her real world, she heard his urging increase. *Come home, sweetheart. I love you.*

"You witch, get out of my way!" Naomi's arm struck out and knocked Genna to the floor with a satisfying thud. With spirit she hadn't known she possessed, Naomi summoned up all she felt for Bryce before she marched over and yanked him toward her, despite his wide eyes. Naomi took hold of him and crushed her mouth down on his.

EXHAUSTED, NAOMI GAZED into her fiancé's terrified eyes. She was home. And there was no place she would rather be than right here in his protective arms.

"Oh, thank God. Thank God. Naomi, Naomi." Smothering her head in kisses, he pulled her tighter, until all she could do was rest her weary head on his chest and cling to him.

"Look at me." Bryce pulled her chin up with a quaking hand. "I'm taking you to the hospital."

"No. I'm okay, really. I'm just shaken up."

Squinting down at her, he smoothed her hair before leaning in to cradle her head.

"What happened to you? I thought I had lost you."

Naomi heard his voice shake and knew how close she had come to losing the disturbing game Nick and his playmate had created. She was the pawn in their cruel plot.

"I heard you, Bryce. It's because of you that I was able to come back." The memory of the cold, hard earth would always remain, but far worse than that was the awareness she had discovered regarding Genna while on the other side. It was the truth, unfortunately, and she would have to tell him.

"Naomi?" Bryce lifted her hands, scrutinizing one and then the other.

"What is it?"

Sitting up, she glanced down at her own dirt-stained hands, turning her ragged fingernails around. She had brought back part of the other terrifying dimension.

"How—"

"Bryce." She clasped his hands firmly, drawing his full attention to her. "I have to tell you something and you need to prepare yourself." The realization had even thrown her off-balance. She would have to choose her next words carefully.

Naomi recalled the sickening, unearthly glow of Genna's gaze back in the other realm. In the end, she knew there was no other way to say it, other than to just come right out with it.

"It's Genna. She's no longer with us." The meaning of her words hadn't quite reached him, she could tell by his questioning eyes. "And Bryce—she's been dead for a while."

Slowly, he released her hands and scooted back on his bottom. Further still, he retreated. "Bryce? Did you hear what I said? She's dead. It's her, Bryce, it's Genna."

Still, he didn't comprehend the words she cried out to him. "Look at me, stop moving away and look at me!"

Bryce's glazed eyes settled on her face and she watched him swallow. "The channeler was right. Nick isn't working alone. He has help. He has Genna."

Saying she was sorry wouldn't do a damn thing and she knew it. Holding him tightly was her only option. Now it was her turn to comfort him. He didn't speak but allowed her to press herself against him.

Standing on his own, Nick was a force to be reckoned with. Teamed up with Genna, they had the power to be indomitable.

CHAPTER TWENTY-FOUR

Naomi

MORE DETERMINED THAN ever to rid herself and this world of the evils of Nick, Naomi hit the street bright and early the next morning. She would pay a visit to both Dr. Bender and Miriam.

Time wasn't on her side, not anymore. Miriam had promised to speed the investigation up on her end, but so far Naomi wasn't impressed with the answers, or lack of, that her friend had turned up.

Dr. Bender would never willingly agree to see Naomi, let alone speak with her if she had called and requested an appointment to speak with him.

As luck would have it, she nearly slammed into the doctor as he opened the glass door to the main entrance. His face dropped as he hurried to compose himself and attempted to scurry off.

"Hey!" Naomi spun on her heels and dodged after him. "Hey! Dr. Bender!"

"You—get away from me." He pointed a finger in Naomi's direction as he quickened his pace.

He wasn't getting away that easily. "Dr. Bender, if you don't speak to me now, I'll have no choice but to call you at home and then discuss my options for reaching you with my friend, Miriam Marty."

At the mention of Miriam's name, his body stilled. Turning in the parking lot to look at Naomi, his shoulders slumped. She had him.

"I promise not to take up too much of your time, but we do need to talk."

"If it's more painkillers you want—"

She had to laugh at that. "You know I didn't come here for medication, Dan. Where can we go to talk?"

He pointed at a bench, far off across the lot. Together, they walked in silence until the wooden seat lay before them.

"Sit," Dr. Bender said.

Naomi took her place beside him and waited for him to begin.

Without prompting, Dan knew exactly where to start the conversation. "Nick used to come see me, but I think you know that already. At first, I think he just needed to sleep. He had some back pain as well as post-traumatic stress and I prescribed some painkillers to help him get some rest."

"Go on," Naomi urged as she leaned closer.

"The only thing that I did wrong was to refill his meds a lot longer than I should have."

"Why would you do that?"

Dr. Bender sighed as he glanced around the lot. "Nick can be very, shall we say, persuasive?"

"Oh, you don't have to tell me that, but how could you just keep giving him the pills?"

"He threatened me." Dan Bender's voice faded.

"What could he possibly have on you? From what I've heard, you've got a reputation for being an outstanding member of this community." It took all Naomi had not to sneer as she commented.

"I'm sure you wouldn't find it a stretch to imagine I had an affair. Several, actually."

"No!" She feigned surprise.

"Don't do that. This is hard enough without your judgments. Nick did some investigating of my personal life, which embarrassingly enough wasn't that difficult to uncover. He found some women whom I've had relations with and threatened to disclose everything to my wife if I didn't keep him in supply of his numerous medications."

Digesting the information, Naomi tried to keep her expression neutral. She merely nodded her head, urging him to continue.

"I know you are probably wondering why I'm admitting this to you, but considering that there's a murder investigation going on . . ."

"I only want the truth. I'm not out to expose your infidelities, regardless of what you may think. Please tell me everything you know about Nick's supply of medication after he went to prison."

"There's nothing to tell, other than passing on the information about Nick's medication to the prison doctor."

"Who is your friend, from what I gather?"

"Yes, I know him. So what?"

"I want to speak with him. Can you arrange that?"

His eyes dropped and a painful expression took over. "Please—"

"If there's nothing to hide, then what is the problem?"

"Why do you have to involve me? Why not just request to speak with the doctor yourself?"

"You know as well as I do that eyebrows would be raised regarding an ordinary citizen requesting to speak with the prison doctor."

"I don't know what you're hoping to find. I'm sorry for what happened here, but it seems to be a case of an accidental, or forgive me for saying, a suicide from overdosing."

"Listen, Dr. Bender. As I'm sure you're aware, Nick and I had no love lost between us. For the sake of what's right here, I need to uncover the truth. I can only say that I have strong reason to believe there was foul play where Nick's death was concerned."

"Why do you care so much if you and Nick were on such bad terms?"

"Let's just say it's complicated."

Dan Bender's eyes searched hers. It was impossible to determine if he was indeed directly involved in Nick's death. For now, she would gather the facts until they gave way to something more credible.

"Have you considered that another inmate was responsible?"

Yes, she had considered the fact that Nick's demise was due to poor relations at the prison. She needed cold, hard facts to get closer to the truth.

"Of course. All of this leads me back to the prison, and namely the doctor who was responsible for Nick."

Reaching into his breast pocket for his cell phone, Naomi watched Dr. Bender fiddle through his contact list. Naomi knew now that she was one step closer to finding her answers.

DAN BENDER AND Dr. Rosen couldn't have been more different in both appearance and attitude. Dr. Rosen, an aging, unassuming man, answered all of her questions without a hitch.

"He claimed he was still in so much pain from his back and of course, I had the previous knowledge of his history with Dr. Bender. I can tell you that the amount of medicine I prescribed was not excessive, nor would it have caused the overdose." Recent autopsy results had confirmed an exorbitant amount of the medication.

"What are your thoughts here, Doctor? Your gut feeling about the true cause of death?"

He didn't so much as blink when he shared his feelings. "I think that Nick got his hands on some additional pain meds and overdosed. What I can't speculate upon is whether or not it was intentional. I'm afraid we'll most likely never know."

Damn. She was back where she started. Miriam had questioned Dr. Rosen previously and uncovered matching facts. Her friend wouldn't be pleased if she learned that Naomi was checking on her work.

"There's nothing else? Nothing?"

Dr. Rosen shook his head, biting on his lip. "I'm afraid not. I'm glad to see that Nick had people who at least cared for him, though."

There was no need to correct the doctor, Naomi figured. Sure, there had once been a time in the distant past where she supposed she had cared for Nick, but that was becoming a very distant memory.

Something about the doctor's comment irked her, though, but she couldn't say why. Naomi pondered it over and decided it was the environment of the cold, hard prison walls bringing her down.

"Thank you, Doctor." She raised a hand to wave good-bye.

Naomi kept her gaze focused on the door as she made her way to the sign-out log on the officer's desk in the main lobby.

Placing her signature among others before her, Naomi lay the pen down and took a step back, slamming into a man behind her.

"I'm sorry!"

"Don't worry." The man moved to the side, dismissing her as he lifted the pen to add his own signature.

People. That's it.

Now she knew what was nagging at her thoughts, just out of reach. The doctor had said the word *people*. Naomi knew that Officer Frank had visited Nick in prison, but what if there was someone else? What if Miriam was misinformed about the visitor log? Or what if someone snuck in here, somehow, under some other pretense, and was directly involved with Nick's death?

The visitors' log returned to her vision. She quickly lifted her cell phone and texted Miriam. Security was tight here and no one could get through the door without showing proper identification. What if, let's say, someone showed their ID but claimed they were here to see another prisoner?

CHAPTER TWENTY-FIVE

Bryce

IT DIDN'T MAKE any sense—but then again, it made all the sense in the world. The sounds, the creaking, the shadows: it could all be explained away by the presence of Genna, or rather, her spirit.

Another mystery which was beginning to become unraveled was Genna returning home to them. Bryce had been sure his ex-wife's recent behavior was out of character and the fact she was a ghost could certainly explain a few things. In a world of the unknown, he pressured his mind to stop wondering how she was able to call him, drive a car, and more. Bryce had learned there were many levels of reality and not so long ago, Naomi's friend Ryan had completed numerous human acts without knowing he had passed.

Did Genna know she was dead? Was she aware that she was playing alongside a very dangerous Nick? He would make it his business to find out and while he was at it, he would do everything in his power to stop her bullying behavior.

He didn't have to wait long to find her, for as if he had summoned her, she now appeared before him in the kitchen of his house. His first thoughts went to Holly, who thankfully was at school for several more hours.

"Genna." Dumbfounded, he wasn't prepared to become tongue-tied as he watched her attractive face transform from stunning, as if lit from within, to a mask of sorrow. A translucent hand groped out, reaching for his cheek. He allowed her hand to remain before he opened his mouth in an attempt to speak.

"She's too strong. I don't have a chance."

What was she talking about? Who was too strong?"

Lightly, Genna stroked his head, cupping his hair in her arms. Closing his eyes, he saw a vision that warmed him from within. He was with both Holly and Naomi and all he could detect was warmth. Warmth and love. Whatever had happened between Naomi and Genna must have provided closure for Genna.

Before he could consider asking what she meant, Genna lifted her feather-light caress from him and stood back before moving in one more time to place a final kiss on his cheek.

Gazing up at the light in her eyes, he shuddered as he strained to hear Genna's last words.

"Your love. It's so powerful. But I can't–I can't help you fight him, because he's strong, so very commanding too. I somehow got so caught up in his wants and needs. I couldn't see clearly anymore."

Bryce pieced together why a soul like Genna would become tangled with Nick's devious spirit. Genna had always been looking for acceptance when it came to her relationships with others, particularly men. Her actions actually stemmed from her own insecurities about herself. An overpowering presence such as Nick would have drawn on her weaknesses and pulled her in. Genna's head had always been too clouded with her own selfish desires to take a step back until it was too late. Apparently, this time was no different.

Crying out did no good. Bryce knew in his heart that Genna and her wisdom of Nick's intentions were gone for good.

Torn between relief that Genna was gone and sadness for the woman he had once thought he loved, he sat at the table, his head in his hands. Holly would never see her mother again; for good or for bad, it was a fact. Genna wouldn't bother them anymore, and he was free to live his life with Naomi. Free, that is, if he could help to rid the world of Nick. He had heeded her warning and considered her words to be brutally honest: Nick's force was formidable, but Bryce had also recently learned that his love for Naomi was incredibly strong as well. Not only was their love powerful, but in Naomi he had found an intensely ardent woman. If Naomi couldn't bring Nick down, then Bryce didn't know who could.

"IF THE FORCE we're dealing with is just Nick, I'm going to be better equipped at dealing with it. When it's just Nick and my mind isn't riddled with visions of you and Genna making a happy family, I can see clearer."

That made sense. If Nick wasn't capable of bringing on such psychological torment on his own, Naomi might stand a chance at defeating him.

"Has anything changed? Do you sense any lessening, any relief at all?"

"It's too soon. Time will tell, I'm sure. This can't hurt, though."

It certainly couldn't. He would take even the slightest bit of promising news right now.

It still nagged at him that he hadn't questioned Genna's disappearance further. "I should have known something was up with Genna. Why didn't I know?" Placing his head in his hands, he wracked his brain. Had he been too caught up in Naomi's troubles or was it the fact that he was just thankful that Genna had been out of his hair?

"Don't blame yourself. You said she was unstable, and let's face it, she was out of your lives when she decided to take off over a year ago. Look, I can ask Miriam if she knows anything about her death."

"Thank you." He considered Naomi's reasoning, She was right, of course. He hadn't heard from Genna long before she met her cruel destiny.

"What did you find out at the prison?" It would help to let go of any guilt right now and focus his energy on helping Naomi.

"Nothing that I didn't already know, but I did have a thought." Naomi shared her idea that maybe their suspect, whoever that may be, may have gotten in under the pretense of visiting another prisoner.

Bryce considered Naomi's words but didn't wish to crush her hopes. What she was saying didn't make a hell of a lot of sense. Honestly, he thought she was grasping at straws but didn't want to hurt her. What purpose would it serve to get in the prison by visiting someone else? It didn't fit. But then a possibility hit him hard.

"Naomi." He reached for her wrists, tightening his grip.

"What is it, Bryce?"

"You might be on the right track here. Let's say someone did enter the prison and somehow got to Nick through someone else on the inside." It made perfect sense to him. If, indeed, there was foul play and that question remained a big *if*.

"Yes. Yes, Bryce. I like the direction you're going in."

Spying traces of hope on her face, he continued. "Following that logic, it would, as you say, make sense to check the visitors' log, or rather have Miriam look into it."

"She's doing so as we speak. Bryce, I have to tell you that I think you might be on to something here."

"I hope so. I want nothing more than for us to get back to where we were, Naomi." He drew closer to her, wrapping his arms around her waist. Kissing her delicate lips, he lost himself momentarily in her.

Abrupt ringing ruined the moment as Naomi turned to look for her phone. "Sorry. I have to take this."

"Of course." He nodded, watching Naomi reach for her cell. Her expression ranged from calm to animated.

Eager to hear about her conversation, Bryce tapped his feet while waiting for Naomi to end the call.

She faced him, her eyes bright. "I have to go. Miriam has something to tell me and she doesn't want to discuss it over the phone."

That could be good or bad. If it was nothing monumental, Miriam would simply tell Naomi what she learned over the phone.

"Do you want me to go with you? I could see—"

"Don't be ridiculous. You shouldn't be late to work on my account. There's been enough of that going on."

She had a point. As much as he hated to leave her to discover new information on her own, he did have a job to go to and although Mark was an understanding boss, Bryce was never one to push the limit.

"Call me as soon as you find anything out."

"You bet."

He kissed her good-bye, excusing himself. Once he stood outside in the sunlight, he leaned against Naomi's front door, breathing in the fresh air. He hoped this mess would soon be placed behind them.

CHAPTER TWENTY-SIX

Naomi

"THAT'S IT? THAT'S what you called me in for?" She didn't understand. Why did Miriam have to call her and get her hopes up?

"Don't you see? The fact that those pages disappeared has to mean something. Papers don't just get up and walk away on their own."

"Yes." Naomi paced the hard linoleum floor beneath her. "I would agree with you on that. So who took it? And where does this leave us?" In her opinion, it was right back to square one. She blew out a harsh breath.

"This tells me that Nick's death was no accident. It can't be coincidental that the visitors' log disappeared. I mean, I checked and this hasn't been known to have happened before, at least not under the current supervision."

Miriam had discovered what Naomi had been sure of all along, what she had been trying to tell her friend. "I already know that Nick's death wasn't an accident. This is what I've been telling you!"

"Relax. I know that you have suspected—"

"Suspected? Hell, I was damn sure and you should have listened. All this time has been wasted. We could have been that much further along." Naomi ran a hand through her thick hair.

Miriam came closer, her finger in the air. "Now listen here. I'm a police officer and I pride myself on being a damn good one. We have procedures to follow, *rules* to abide by."

She was right. Just because Naomi had the ability to see and speak with the supernatural didn't mean that everyone could understand. "I'm sorry. You're right. I'm anxious to finish this."

Staring down at her feet, Naomi sighed, wishing she could go back and retract her words. Lately it seemed she was upsetting the ones she loved most.

"I get that, I do. I understand your need to speed things up and I will do my best to act quickly. I'm trying to gather the footage from the camera located near the sign-in desk. I'm not sure if they would even keep it this long. Now is there anyone you can think of, anyone at all that would wish Nick dead or would benefit from his death? Think, Naomi, think."

Funny thing was, she had considered possible suspects or lack of, for that matter, for a while. Nick didn't know that many people, and besides Uncle Frank, who else would have possible reach into the prison?

"I don't know, Miriam. I don't know."

"Well, let's be objective here, if you will. Nick has made several enemies. There's Maggie, but she's dead, so that leaves—"

Mr. and Mrs. Fields' faces popped into her head. Miriam couldn't possibly think they would have anything to do with this.

"No—"

"I'm not saying they could, believe me, I'm not. I'm playing devil's advocate here. Someone is bound to question them."

Her friend was proving to be almost as skillful at reading her thoughts as Bryce was. She had to tell Miriam about Dr. Bender's admission right now and she was surprised it had even slipped her mind.

"Listen, there is something I need to tell you, but I'm asking that you not use it unless necessary." She didn't give a crap about Dr. Bender's feelings, but wished to spare his wife embarrassment. Hell, now that she considered it, the wife might be better off knowing about all of his conquests—that way she could leave the bastard—but it wasn't her call to make.

"Spill it."

"I went to speak with Dr. Bender."

Miriam flipped her hands through the air. "Again?"

"Yes," Naomi mumbled.

"Against my wishes? If you were anyone else and if you didn't have a crazy ass ghost on your tail, I'd bring you in for obstructing justice."

Naomi didn't feel that was a fair assessment of her actions. Technically, she wasn't hindering justice, she was actually contributing to it. Knowing now wasn't the time to discuss semantics, she kept her lips sealed.

"Well?"

Clearing her throat, Naomi told Miriam of Dr. Bender's confession. Uncharacteristically speechless, Naomi waited Miriam's silence out. Feeling a slight sweat starting to break, Naomi paced the room.

"Wow. I cannot believe he actually admitted that to you. I don't even know what to say. I mean, from what I know of Dan, I wouldn't have thought he was capable of this."

Blowing out a huff of air, Naomi found it a challenge to contain herself. Once upon a time, not so long ago, when they had been investigating Maggie's death, Miriam had called her naïve. Now who was the one being naïve?

Naomi opened her mouth to speak her mind, but thought better as she didn't want to interrupt her friend while she was concentrating. "But what does this mean? Do you seriously think Dan Bender would *kill* Nick in order to ensure nobody found out about his affairs?"

She opened her mouth again, but then heard Miriam start to ramble. "Then why tell *you* so easily? Why bring it out in the open and risk his wife discovering if he had gone through such lengths to cover it up?"

Naomi attempted to speak once more, but Miriam spoke over her, drowning out her words. "And of course he wouldn't want his wife to find out, especially considering the old family money—"

"Wait. What? What did you say about family money?"

"His wife. Mrs. Bender comes from old family money. Her relatives were practically royalty down South."

She scrunched her nose. "Down South? Where?"

"Florida. Her family is practically celebrity status in their hometown."

"But it doesn't make sense. You're right, he gave up the affair information pretty quickly."

"Because maybe that's exactly what he wants us to think. That the only thing he's responsible for was indiscretion." Miriam's gaze flitted around the room and rested back on Naomi. "He's on my list. As much as this is going to piss Phil off, Dan's a suspect as far as I'm concerned." She shook her head before adding, "But that's really none of Phil's business, I suppose."

"And Mr. and Mrs. Field?" Naomi had to make sure they were ruled out.

"You know as well as I do that neither could harm a fly. Don't worry, I certainly won't be the one to bring up their names and hopefully no one else will even consider them."

That was a relief. Naomi would call them or stop by, though, just to see if they knew of anyone else who might seek revenge on Nick.

"I got it covered. Let me do my job, Naomi."

"What?"

"*I* will stop by and speak with Maggie's parents. Got it?"

Saluting to her friend, she stifled back a grin. "Yes, ma'am." As she turned to leave, she remembered the favor she needed from Miriam.

"Can you confirm the death of a woman?"

"Sure, and who would that be?" Naomi was met with a smirk.

Naomi shared the information that had unfolded with Genna. It seemed that Miriam was slowly becoming accustomed to ghostly spirits as she took in the latest turn of events without batting an eye.

"Life with you is never dull, is it?" Miriam slapped her shoulder and then retreated back to her computer for a few minutes. Naomi spent the time wandering around Miriam's office, glancing at the certificates and photographs on her wall. Heading back to Miriam's desk, she took at seat while waiting. A framed photo on Miriam's desk caught her attention. Each time she and Phil had met, she was reminded of Ryan. It was no different looking at the photo of Miriam and Phil, their arms wrapped around each other, smiles wide, set against the river.

"Where was this taken?" She held up the photo, turning it around in her hand.

"Huh?" Miriam looked up from her computer and grinned at the picture. "Oh, that was a few months ago. We were at that new restaurant upstate a bit, you know, the Italian place that opened with the fabulous views."

"Yes, it's right near the prison. I told Bryce we should try it out." They had been so busy, she had nearly forgotten. Also, it was a bit of a hike to get there.

"You should definitely go if you get the chance. It's worth the trip. I had to go up to the prison anyway, so he tagged along and we went on the way home."

The image of Miriam dragging her date through the prison earned a laugh from Naomi. "You sure know how to show a guy a good time, my friend."

With the flick of Miriam's hand, her grin expanded as she sent a wad of paper flying in Naomi's direction. "You know it."

The momentary distraction eased her mind, but soon Naomi remembered Genna. "Did you find anything?"

"Here's your girl. She was initially tagged as a 'Jane Doe' until recently, since there was no ID found on her." Miriam spun her computer so that it was facing Naomi. She was met with a spreadsheet-type document. Even squinting, she had a difficult time reading the words.

"The police should have notified Bryce, but because of his recent move, they must not have found him easily." Miriam glanced at Naomi.

"Tell me what it says."

"Well, it looks like Genna was traveling back East when she and her companion stopped at a roadside hotel.

It says here that it was homicide. Her body was found the next morning when the maid came in the room to clean. Her boyfriend was arrested for murdering her. Witnesses claim to have heard screaming the night before."

"That's awful." Her heart went out to Genna. As much as she hadn't liked Genna, she wouldn't wish that on anyone.

A sudden thought hit her as a possible, if not probable, scenario came to mind. What if Genna had left an abusive boyfriend to try to come back to Holly? Or Holly and Bryce? Genna had, in fact, made it back, just not in the state they would have assumed. And those dreams? Dreams mimicked reality, even if they were induced by ghosts. Her stomach dropped as a queasiness came over her.

"SO BASICALLY WE'RE still clueless except that now Miriam believes me when I tell her foul play was involved. Oh, and Genna's death was most definitely confirmed."

Bryce's exhale came across loudly and clearly through the phone. He listened without a word as Naomi told him the few details they had discovered about Genna's death.

"I'm sorry, Bryce. I know this can't be easy for you to hear." She was, after all, the mother of his child.

"It's not. Of course it's not. I wish this whole thing had played out differently."

"So do I." Neither of them spoke about the possibilities of what could have happened had Genna made it back alive to her daughter. Would she have been as aggressive in nature as she had been in spirit form?

They would never know, and that was a blessing of sorts, she supposed.

"Whew, Naomi. Where does that leave us? What are you thinking now?"

Naomi wished he could see her smile as she recalled a fond memory in which both she and Bryce had sat in her house burning the midnight oil, trying to solve Maggie's death and give the ghost closure. There had been sheets of paper all around, a haphazard timeline of events leading up to Maggie's death.

"Remember that night when we wrote down everything we could think of relating to Maggie's mystery?"

"You mean when I forced you to sit down and write everything on paper? That was my idea, you know."

Even now, he had to take credit for the brilliant idea. A smirk set in as she recalled his famous words. "And you said—and I quote—*Just dreams? You're the writer here. Use your imagination.*"

"That's right, Naomi. That's right."

"So?"

"What are you waiting for? I'll put on the coffee."

CHAPTER TWENTY-SEVEN

Naomi

PAPERS COVERED THE table, but they were no closer to finding an answer than they were when they had acted out this scenario with Maggie. Yes, Naomi was the writer and she was trying to force her imagination to take hold but it wasn't budging. Not this time. Who could have taken the log at the prison? It would make sense to assume it was a job from the inside, but in that case, why steal the log?

No.

No.

No.

It had to be someone from the outside then. A very clever someone.

They had been at it for hours and she felt exhaustion creeping in. Judging from Bryce's shadowed eyes, she knew he felt the same way. Luckily, Bryce's friend John had come to visit and offered to watch Holly for a few hours so they could try to get some answers.

Time was ticking away. Quickly. Too quickly and they both knew it. Neither would say what the other was thinking.

"Good night, Bryce. Get some sleep." Naomi leaned over and placed her arms around his neck. Inhaling his aftershave, she wanted to bottle the scent to keep him beside her through the night.

"I don't want to leave you." His broken whisper tickled her neck.

Pulling herself from his embrace, she saw his eyes mist over. He broke her heart, this brave, strong man of hers. This was something he had little to no control over and she knew it was killing him to watch her so helpless against Nick.

"I promised you back at the hotel that I would be by your side, that I would do better."

"And you have." She cupped his face in her shaking hands. Each time they were together lately, she found herself slightly melancholy. "Are you kidding? You and I are in this together, you're the strength I pulled back from the other side that night. Without you calling for me, I wouldn't have made it."

"I know, I know. It's so hard. I can't bring Holly here, but please know that I would never leave your side if it wasn't for our daughter."

It melted her heart to hear him speak the words aloud. *Our daughter.* A serious look crossed his face as he set his angular jaw tight.

"I don't know how it could have slipped my mind, but something else happened that weekend we were away at Cape Florence. It was the last night of the trip, after you and Holly had fallen asleep."

His pause was audible. Naomi's pulse sped up as she prepared herself for his next words.

"That woman, the ghost, Emily Summers. She came to me." Bryce gazed down at the floor. She lifted his chin so they were staring eye to eye.

"Go on. What is it? What did Emily do?" Blonde hair and unearthly beauty filled her head.

"She told me not to let you down, that you're safe with me." A lone tear slid down his cheek and she kissed it away.

"Don't do this, don't get emotional on me or I'm going to lose it." Her own tears flowed, mixing with his as Bryce pulled Naomi closer.

"Look at us. We're a mess." Bryce laughed through his tears. He then cleared his throat, pulling back. "What if I let her down?"

"What you really mean is, what if you let *me* down." Naomi watched him struggle with his emotions.

"Yes. What am I going to do then?"

"You're not going to do anything because nothing is going to happen to me or us, for that matter, you hear? I refuse to let some loser of an ex-boyfriend—did you hear that, Nick?" She paused before continuing, "I refuse to let him ruin me."

Bryce nodded his head, his eyes focused on Naomi. "Genna told me you were strong. You defeated her, Naomi. I have faith in you."

"*We* defeated her, Bryce. *Our love* brought her down and we can do it again."

Sighing, he clamped his hands around her head and then pressed his lips to hers. She didn't rush the kiss, but rather savored it, drinking him in. For all her courageous talk, she had to admit that each time she saw Bryce, touched him, she worried it could be the last.

TONIGHT, SHE DREAMED of Ryan. He stood before her, mere inches away. His quirky smile warmed her heart, but it wasn't directed toward her. Maggie was the one he directed his attention to. Maggie.

Naomi cried out, projecting her voice the best she could, but he looked right through her. Tears welled up, forcing her to turn away from him.

Lucidity came over her, as she had the ability to step back and see that she was merely dreaming this time. Why now? Why the lucid dream?

Realizing her ache for touching Ryan, for seeing him again, was a growing need, she took off, running for him in her dream state.

Closer, and closer still, she was almost upon him. He stood, transfixed, bright-blue eyes wide. He wanted to see her too, she could tell by his gentle smile, the warmth coming over his features.

Almost there. She was almost in his arms. Sweeping her feet up, she jumped into his waiting arms, her heart filling with a love so deep, so warm. Her body fell to the ground with an audible thud. Rubbing at her aching shoulder, she pulled herself upright and searched the open field for him. Seconds ago, the sky sparkled bright and sunny. Now dark clouds moved in, heading for her until she could see nothing except Maggie's innocent face, a single tear falling as the spirit closed her eyes.

What the hell was that? Naomi pulled her knees up and hugged her chest to them. The dream left her with fresh tears on her cheeks. Ryan would never snub her, would he?

One thing she had learned from all of the paranormal events cascading around her was that dreams were sometimes just that, dreams. But other times? Now she knew that some nightmares were based on reality and worse still, some predicted her future.

From the corner of her sleep-stained eyes, she saw a flash of a woman. It was her—that dark-haired woman from one of her recent dreams. Piercing blue eyes flashed from across the room. Sucking in her breath, Naomi felt a sensation not unlike the one she had the last time she witnessed this surreal young woman. Her ragged breath burned her throat. Just out of reach, Naomi felt as if she should know this woman, her mind so close to pinpointing her importance, but then all thoughts blanked and she couldn't be certain her mind wasn't playing tricks on her.

Zelda pounced onto her bed as if she sensed Naomi needed her. The cat snuggled her warm body against Naomi. Pressing closer to her feline companion, Naomi found solace in the rare moment. Not so long ago Naomi had been carefree, going out with Amy on blind dates, before this ghost business had begun.

How many relationships had she neglected? Naomi would call Amy today and see if she wanted to meet up for lunch. She also made a mental note to stop by and visit Maggie's parents. Since Nick had made his presence abundantly clear, her time spent with the Fields had suffered as well. And Holly? She and Holly could be building memories . . . Naomi pulled her covers up over her head and allowed a moment of pity to come over her.

Stop feeling sorry for yourself and get your act together.

Hearing the words clearly, Naomi sat upright, gasping. She was alone in the room, with only Zelda by her side. But then, her cat did a remarkable thing. Zelda stared at the doorway, eyes planted squarely on a spot just outside the door to her bedroom. The cat then squealed delightfully and bounded off with the speed of a wildcat. Naomi cocked her head and followed the increasing sounds from downstairs.

She had heard those exact noises before, she was sure of it. As Naomi drew closer, she realized where the clatter was coming from.

Naomi knew exactly who was making the racket and what was going on. Her heart filled with warmth as she took in the scene before her.

Cabinets flew wildly, opening and shutting. With glee, Naomi witnessed Zelda at her happiest. Her cat, of course, had been at her most playful when she and Maggie were playing. Before Maggie visualized before her, Naomi clasped her hands together, savoring this extraordinary feeling.

Holding her breath, Naomi allowed herself to be consumed by Maggie's presence. The blonde's natural beauty shone through as she extended a hand for Naomi to grab hold of.

Words couldn't begin to touch the bond these two women continued to share. Naomi basked in Maggie's light, waiting for the spirit to attempt to speak. Communication had been challenging until Naomi had freed the spirit's soul not so long ago.

"I'm trying, Naomi. He's overwhelming."

"I know." She didn't need Maggie to help her realize that, what she needed was guidance. "What should I do? Where do I turn?'

Maggie shook her long mane of hair, tears spilling from her tragic blue eyes. "He won't, he won't let me. He's blocking—"

Her message came in spurts and stops. What was Maggie trying to say? Nick wouldn't let her help? She could imagine him blocking any attempts at rescuing Naomi. Is that what Maggie meant?

"Yes, I can see that. How do I stop him? What does he want? Do you know who killed him?"

"I can't—I'm not able. Pay attention to the small details."

Straining to hear Maggie, she wasn't sure she had heard her correctly. *Pay attention to the small details?* What did that mean? Apparently they were right back to communicating through riddles. This was making Naomi crazy. Why couldn't Maggie help her? Why was she blocked? Wasn't she as strong as Nick? Couldn't her spirit attempt to overpower him?

Couldn't Maggie at least try?

"Maggie—please! For me, for Ryan. I'm sure he wants you to help me." Ryan. Where was Ryan? The recent nightmare plagued her mind, invading her train of thought. It struck her that the dream couldn't have been just a nightmare. If the dream held no meaning, Ryan would have been here, standing beside Maggie.

"Where is he, Maggie? Where's Ryan?"

The apparition dissipated as quickly as she had arrived.

Maggie. Where are you?

Even Zelda's form slumped in displeasure. What could she have possibly done to cause Ryan's distance?

Concern had etched Maggie's face when Naomi questioned Ryan's whereabouts. She was sure of it.

And what had Maggie advised? Forcing her thoughts back to the ghost's comment, she recalled her exact phrase: *Pay attention to the small details.*

Did the comment mean to look around and question everything around her? That would prove to be extremely challenging. Possibilities swirled around her. Dr. Bender, of course, was her number one suspect, but even he was on shaky ground with her. Lots of details there didn't make sense.

Small details. Small details. Her head pounded, filling up too fast with a plethora of information.

CHAPTER TWENTY-EIGHT

Bryce

THEY WERE MISSING something. Something monumental, he was sure of it. When all of the bare facts slapped them in the face last night, he still couldn't see it.

He and Naomi were too close to the situation; that had to be it. So what was the next move then? How do you distance yourself in order to see the big picture? How do you forget all you see around you and attempt to view the world with fresh eyes?

The answer hit him instantly. What else would you do when you're asking for advice, but to tell an outsider, someone with little knowledge of your current dilemma. Someone whom you don't speak with on a regular basis. It would be even better if that person didn't think he was insane for bringing up ghost stories.

Jackson and Kristen.

Of course. Why hadn't he thought about this before?

Fumbling through his wallet, he located the business card which proudly displayed *Jane's Ending* and the appropriate book logo. His fingers couldn't have punched in the number fast enough.

When a man's voice answered, he felt his breath catch. At least he wouldn't have to wait long to ask for the favor.

"Jackson?"

"Yes, Jackson here. Who's calling?"

"It's Bryce, we were just at Jane's Ending."

"Of course. How are Naomi and Holly doing?"

Bryce felt touched that Jackson would remember their names. One of the trademarks of a successful business owner was recalling the small details to make their customers feel important.

"I know this might sound like a strange request, but do you have a couple of minutes to listen to me and give me your thoughts on something?"

"Um—sure. Give me five, ten minutes? I'll track Kristen down and we'll put you on speaker phone."

"Sounds perfect. Thanks, Jackson. I'm asking you guys because I know you've been through something similar."

"Hey, no worries. I guess you could call us ghost experts if you want. I kind of like the sound of it." Jackson chuckled and then excused himself to find Kristen.

The few minutes it took waiting for Jackson and Kristen to call him back gave him time to think. *Small details.* The phrase came to Bryce as strange feelings swept over him. Jackson's attention to detail had him thinking. He and Naomi were wracking their brains trying to solve this mystery surrounding them. They were looking at the big picture. Perhaps what they needed to do was step back and focus on the lesser details.

Between the impending conversation with Jackson and Kristen coupled with focusing on the small details of Nick's death, Bryce figured he might be that much closer to uncovering the truth.

Jackson's number flashed on the screen of his phone, breaking into his thoughts momentarily. Grabbing his cell, he prepared to tell not just some hurried details, but the long version of Nick's death to the owners of Jane's Ending.

THE GRACEFUL COUPLE couldn't have been more courteous and helpful. Not only did they listen to his long-winded tale of Maggie, Ryan, and Nick, but they seemed to *get it*. They had a true handle on the paranormal. And they also offered a fresh perspective, which was precisely what Bryce had been looking for.

Jackson wondered who had the most to gain from Nick's death while Kristen figured whoever was responsible likely committed the crime for emotional reasons—for revenge, perhaps, or even sorrow. Since he and Naomi had already considered reasons of malice, Bryce focused now on the emotional angle.

Sorrow was most definitely an interesting twist now that he considered it. But it brought him back to all of the same questions. Who would be that devastated by Maggie's death? The obvious answer was her parents. But that was utterly ridiculous in his opinion. Maggie's parents were among the sweetest people he had ever known.

Who would be crushed by Ryan's death? His parents were no longer around, so that left who? The only friend he had known the man to have was Naomi.

Naomi? A chill coursed through his veins as he shook his head, dismissing the unwelcome intrusion. Naomi would never harm another human being, ever. No—he wouldn't allow himself to even entertain the idea. Naomi was the most genuine soul he had encountered in his life.

Who else did that leave? The only family Ryan had was his brother, Phil. And come on, Phil was dating Miriam, the very officer in charge of Nick's case. Miriam would have to be blind not to notice something was off.

A twisted vision of Naomi's face pushed through his mind. It was the very image he had tried so hard to repel. *Naomi hated Nick for so many reasons. He killed two of the people she loved most. Nick messed with her mind in life and in death.*

No! Not even if a gun was held to her head. And she would have to be the best actress around to pull off her conflicting emotions and pure dedication to the task of finding Nick's murderer.

Was this what Naomi had felt when Genna had consumed her mind? Piercing thoughts, poisonous images she couldn't shut off?

Knowing his own mind wouldn't allow such garbage to enter, he grimaced. *I will not allow you to mess with my head, Nick. I love her and trust her. Go away. Go away. Go away!*

Droplets of sweat oozed down his back as Bryce fought to catch his breath. The wave of uncertainty disappeared, replaced by a renewed confidence in Naomi. What had he been sucked into back there? Nick's reach had power, but Bryce's love for his fiancée was even more potent.

LATER THAT NIGHT, Naomi called him to say good night. He shared his recent conversation with the owners of *Jane's Ending*. She listened intently, interjecting only a few comments here and there. From the fading quality in her voice, he knew she was feeling down.

It wouldn't due to have her waning, not now when there was too much to lose.

When he had thought Naomi was prepared to end the call, she commented about seeing Maggie and shared the ghost's advice to focus on the small details.

"Her exact words were, *pay attention to the small details.* What do you think she means, Bryce?"

"Funny you should say that." He scratched at his scalp. "During my conversation with Jackson earlier, he asked how you and Holly were doing and I thought that it was important for a business owner to recall details about a person. It got me thinking about Nick's murder."

"Amazing."

"Yeah, I would have to admit it is pretty amazing that I considered exactly what Maggie had been conveying to you." *I mean, what were the chances?* Again, Bryce was awed by this bond between Naomi, Maggie, and now himself.

He shared Kristen's angle on the suspect having emotional ties to either Maggie or Ryan.

"But that leaves just Mr. and Mrs. Field or Phil. They're both preposterous possibilities. I mean, Phil and Ryan had even lost touch there for a while. We're back at square one—again. How is that I can't think of one other person who loved Ryan, or Maggie for that matter, enough to become so utterly devastated that they would act on it and commit murder? I mean, that would take someone who both hated Nick that much and loved Ryan or Maggie in a way that they could not recover."

He had nothing to add to her comment because he had pondered the very same inquiry moments ago.

There was no one. No one else who fit the mold.

"Bryce—"

Because he was attuned to Naomi like nobody else, when he heard the strain in her voice, he was certain she had just uncovered the thought that he had worked so hard to eradicate earlier.

"Naomi—"

"Oh my God, Bryce. What if—"

"What? It was you? That's the craziest idea yet. Naomi, you're not a murderer."

"But that would also explain why Nick is torturing me. He—he doesn't want anything from me other than pure revenge." Naomi sobbed out the sputtering words.

He wasn't having this. She needed to stop this line of thinking or she would truly go mad.

"Listen to me and pay attention to every single word I say. Do. Not. Go. There. Even if you question yourself, I will not. You couldn't hurt anyone."

"Not even in the name of love? Avenging Maggie's and Ryan's senseless accidents?"

Damn. He should be there, chasing away her absurd thoughts. "No, Naomi. Not even then."

"What if it was me that killed him?"

"I'm not entertaining this conversation. Take a deep breath and relax. You would have had to get your hands on medication, get into the prison, somehow smuggle the drugs and get someone to give it to him. Come on now. You couldn't have done all that. Why wouldn't you remember? You couldn't have blacked it all out."

Silence gave way to a long sigh. "You're right. I'm so desperate to finish this with Nick that I'm even blaming myself. I need a good night's sleep, Bryce, that's all."

"Yes, you do and when this is over, I'm taking you away on a nice, long vacation."

She chuckled softly. "That would be our honeymoon, which reminds me that I should be planning our wedding." Her voice trailed off, a sadness coming through.

His mind went directly back in time, to that special day when he had proposed to Naomi by cliffs, right near the tree with their initials freshly carved beside Maggie and Ryan's own initials. So much sadness had transpired before and since then.

"Nobody would be capable of planning a wedding with this circus going on around us. It will come in time. Focus on this now, Naomi, and we'll deal with planning the most beautiful wedding there ever was when you get rid of Nick."

Promising Naomi he would stop by in the morning before work, he swore he would never tell Naomi of the horrifying manifestation that had taken hold of his mind moments before she called.

CHAPTER TWENTY-NINE

Naomi

SLOWLY, SHE WAS going to drive herself over the edge of madness if she didn't silence her overwrought mind. Bryce was right. In every sense of the word. It was ludicrous to suspect she had the ability to murder Nick. Crazier still to imagine she could have blacked out the entire scheme.

If only she could clear her mind and have some peace. It wasn't just the stress of Nick plaguing her; it was bills, deadlines, appointments, and everything in between that haunted her day and night. Her overdriven mind did have one purpose though: it helped her to investigate the possibilities hanging over her.

Jules had called earlier to inform her of her latest galleys, which were now available to review. This last step before publishing always excited her, even now. The galleys might be just what she needed right now.

Feeling a bit lighter, Naomi stretched out the kinks in her back and fumbled with her laptop. Her desktop was littered with papers that should have been neatly stacked in her bin. Zelda was up to her usual tricks, it appeared. Try as she might, Naomi couldn't control her cat from jumping up and messing around with the items on her desk. The darn cat knew exactly what she was doing, for when Naomi caught her in the act, Zelda would screech and hightail it out of the room.

Squinting her eyes at one of the papers, she noticed a recent book contract that should have been properly filed away. She reached over and opened her small filing cabinet to file the paperwork.

Before closing the cabinet, some photographs caught her eye. Picking up the loose pictures, Naomi figured she should get a small photo album to store them in. Peering down at one picture which captured Miriam's wide smile perfectly, she recalled the day she had taken it. They had been ice-skating at the local mall. She and Miriam had been at the mall shopping and having lunch when they decided it would be a goof to go skating. The mall's indoor rink was large enough that Naomi could hang on to the side railing while getting lost in the crowd. Miriam had shown off her stellar skills with a whopper grin, which Naomi had caught with her cell camera.

A pang deep in her gut registered, causing Naomi to gasp aloud. It was the picture. Not this one, but the recent photo of Miriam and Phil. At the time, she failed to see the relevance of the setting.

Miriam had stated she had brought Phil to the prison while she stopped in quickly before going to the restaurant. Phil had been at the prison not so long ago, as recently as a couple of months ago when the log had disappeared. Had Miriam left him alone at any point?

Naomi's fingers shook as she grabbed her cell and hit Miriam's name on her contact list. *Come on. Answer the phone. Answer it.*

"What's up?"

Whew. "Miriam. Thank goodness. Listen, I have a question I need to ask and please don't get upset. Promise me."

"I can't promise that. What have you been up to now?"

Oh, this wasn't starting off well. "Remember, what I'm about to tell you is a *theory,* just a theory."

"Spit it out, Naomi. I have work to do."

"Okay—remember that photograph of you and Phil outside of the restaurant?"

Her friend mumbled acknowledgment and she continued. "You mentioned the other day that Phil had tagged along at the prison, right?"

A lengthy pause filled the air with tension. "I don't think I like where you're going with this, Naomi. What are you getting at?" Miriam snapped.

"Did you leave him alone at all? Even for a minute?"

"Huh? I—this is ridiculous! First you go off investigating on your own and now Phil is a suspect? *Phil?*"

"I know it sounds like a reach, but just consider it. I mean, he would have motive. Let's face it."

"Yeah? And guess what? So would you. I didn't want to bring this up before, but hell, anything goes now, I suppose."

Naomi's pulse sped as she struggled to breathe. "Don't say that."

"It's crazy, right? Of course I know you wouldn't do such a thing, that's why I haven't questioned you. Don't ask me to do that to Phil, Naomi. Don't you dare."

So Miriam wasn't open to the possibility. Fine. Naomi was used to working on her own anyway. "Sorry, you're right, I guess."

"You guess?"

"You're right. It's an absurd idea. Sorry."

"I mean, you're basically saying I'm a stupid fool if I'm following your logic here. I'm a cop, Naomi, a cop. If something was going on with Phil related to this case, don't you think I would pick up on it?"

"Yes. Yes—of course you would. I'm reaching and grasping for anything I can think of, I'm afraid."

Naomi said the right things to Miriam, but she wasn't about to let this go without at least looking into it. On her own.

"Now that all of the stupidity is out of the way, are you going to come by and pick up your jacket?"

Shoot. Miriam had reminded her several times over the past week that she had left her jacket at her house the last time she stopped by. It had slipped her mind with everything going on.

"Yeah, I'll stop by soon. I have another light jacket meanwhile."

"Fine. But, I know you and you'll be looking for it and won't remember where it is if you wait too much longer."

"I'll swing by when I can."

"Good. Now promise me you won't do anything stupid today." Miriam's firm command came through loud and clear.

"Promise." And like she had done so many times as a child, Naomi crossed her fingers behind her back before disconnecting the call.

IT ENDED UP being nearly impossible to formulate a plan to see if Phil had taken the visitors' log. What was she supposed to do, just waltz into the prison and show Phil's picture around, asking if he looked familiar and had gotten into their paperwork?

Seething, Naomi thought the only other plan of action would be to try to somehow get into Phil's apartment without him knowing and snoop around. Talk about pissing off Miriam. Naomi could only imagine her friend's reaction if she were caught in the act.

If only Ryan showed himself and offered up some advice here. It was his brother, after all. Ryan would know if Phil was capable of murder.

Something in the air shifted and a slight chill filled the room. Glancing around slowly, Naomi watched as several books from her bookshelf crashed to the floor.

"Who is that?"

Silence. Whoever it was didn't wish to be revealed. A startled Zelda bounded off around the corner, her eyes gleaming at Naomi.

"I know, sweetie. You never quite get used to it, do you?"

Back to the final galleys it was, although the thought of Phil never wandered far from her mind as she reread each and every word of her manuscript forward and backwards.

At last, Naomi reached the bittersweet words: *The end.* Satisfied that her manuscript was in tip-top shape, she typed out a quick email and attached the galleys. Jules would be thrilled she had finished the work and Naomi was actually a few days ahead of her deadline, although she had no idea how that could have happened with all the chaos swirling around her.

Sitting back in her chair, Naomi placed her hands behind her head and reveled in the sweetness of completing another book. She might just crack open that new bottle of wine she had been saving for a special occasion. Yes, as a matter of fact, what better time than now to celebrate? Before she even had a chance to stand up, her cell phone rang.

Wondering what Miriam could want so soon after their previous conversation, Naomi thought maybe it could be some breaking news about the case.

"Hey. What have you got?" Her upbeat tone reflected her rare mood. Unfortunately, the ambience she had worked so hard to create dissipated in an instant.

"Naomi—get your ass to my house right now."

Well. She considered asking what it was she had done, but figured at this point it could be most anything. Without saying a word, Naomi ended the call and grabbed her shoes.

What now? What could it possibly be now?

CHAPTER THIRTY

Naomi

BEFORE SHE COULD place her hand on Miriam's front door to knock, a swift hand reached out and grabbed her.

"Wow. Hello to you, too." What had gotten into Miriam? Whatever Naomi had gotten into, whatever toes she had stepped on, couldn't be that bad.

Standing before her was a pissed off—make that an extremely pissed off—Miriam. Her normally smooth hair stuck out here and there, giving her a bedhead appearance. Mascara was smeared under her blue eyes.

"Have you been crying?" Naomi moved closer to inspect her friend's face. Hard to tell if Miriam was now sad or angry as hell, Naomi figured it was best to give Miriam some space.

"How could you? I mean—to leave this out?" Miriam flung a wad of papers at her, which hit her and flew into disarray on the floor by her feet.

"What the heck is that and what the hell has gotten into you?" Naomi's eyes went wide as her heart thumped wildly in her chest. Pieces of the puzzle started fitting together.

"Is that—?"

"You bet it is. Care to guess who our little surprise visitor is?"

"I—Phil?" Naomi squeaked.

Miriam's eyes clouded, a storm approaching. "No—not Phil! It's not Phil!"

"Then I don't understand. Please—" Sweat pooled down Naomi's lower back as nausea rose in her stomach.

"It's you, Naomi! You!"

Shock riveted through her core as Naomi stepped back, right against the cold countertop as Miriam pounced in on her, teeth bared.

"You're scaring me, Miriam. Stop, just stop and talk to me!" Naomi held her head in her hands, attempting to drown out the screaming in her own head.

"You'd better speak up and tell me what the hell you were doing visiting Johnny Clarke," Miriam seethed. "On more than one occasion."

Johnny Clarke? She didn't know anyone by the name of Johnny Clarke. "Who's Johnny Clarke?"

Cryptic laughter fell from Miriam's lips. "Oh, you're good. I'll give you that. You had *me* fooled. Guess I'm the naïve one this time, aren't I?"

Ignoring the rambling, Naomi pushed against her fear. "I asked you who Johnny Clarke is. Tell me."

Placing her hands on her slender hips, Miriam's eyes rose to the ceiling. "Goes by the name of Crackers, synonymous for certifiably insane."

"Crackers?" Truly baffled, Naomi shook her head and then focused on the white sea of papers strewn on the floor. Picking up the papers, one at a time, she zeroed in on some of the names. None of them looked familiar.

"February sixth, February seventh, February tenth…"

"What?" Naomi's head spun, picking up momentum as she attempted to tune out the strange dates thrown at her. Searching for the inmate named Johnny Clarke, otherwise known as Crackers, her breath hitched in her throat as a trembling finger touched the log where the prisoner's name was listed.

"It—it says—"

"I know what it says. It's your signature! Now tell me what business you have with the most dangerous man in the prison and why you kept it from me."

Images, faces, names, and dates came hard and fast, rummaging through her mind. "No. No. No!"

Miriam's eyes went wide as Naomi reached for the counter to steady her buckling knees. Miriam's garbled shouts came from all directions. Vomit rose up in her throat; swallowing it down, Naomi collided with the closing darkness.

"NAOMI. NAOMI." THE distant voice called for her. Fighting the urge to open her eyes, Naomi wished for nothing but to sink back into the oblivion. Persistent shouting gave way to shaking. Oh, if only the heavy pounding in her skull would stop.

"Naomi. Wake up, talk to me." This time, recognition came over Naomi as she knew who was crying out for her and rocking her.

The blinding light made it too painful to open her eyes for more than a second. "My head—"

"Thank God. Thank God."

Miriam squeezed her body against Naomi, pressing tighter and tighter still. Now on top of her pulsing head, she couldn't breathe. "My head hurts."

"I know, you hit your head going down. Thank God you're alive."

Gazing up at Miriam's face, it all came crashing back. The log.

Johnny Clarke, aka Crackers.

She had killed Nick. She was the murderer.

"Now sit still. I was just about to call the ambulance. Do you need to go to the hospital?"

"Slow down. No, no hospital. Miriam, what have I done?"

"I don't know, I just don't know." Silence fell upon them as Miriam kissed the top of her head.

"We'll figure this out. I'm going to help you, I'll protect you." Miriam's fresh tears spilled on Naomi's head as she rocked her gently.

"Don't cry. And no, I can't let you risk your job. Whatever I did, I'll turn myself in."

"You really don't remember anything, do you?" Miriam moved her head back to face Naomi.

"Not a thing. But it must have been me. What would I be doing visiting a man named Crackers?" Straining to think clearly only served to hurt her aching skull more.

"Nothing good, I can tell you that. Right now, you concentrate on getting better. I'm going to grab some ice for your head. Stay there."

Dizziness swept over her, causing Naomi to grab at the table leg behind her. "Oh—"

"Don't get up. I think I should call a doctor." Miriam assessed her, squinting her eyes.

"No doctor. I'll be okay. Miriam, don't ignore the eight-hundred pound gorilla. What am I going to do?"

The freezer door slammed shut as Miriam scurried back to Naomi. Sliding down to the floor beside Naomi, her friend wrapped her in a hug. "I don't know, sweetie."

Where had Miriam even located the missing log? And what about the camera footage? "Where did you find the log?"

"That's the weird thing. It was found in a pile of papers inside of the desk in the lobby of the prison. We had searched there I don't know how many times."

"I put it back? Did I do that?" When would she have had the time to sneak in there and put it back without being noticed? No, this didn't make any sense.

"Apparently it found its way back. Why you would choose to incriminate yourself is beyond me."

"Guilt. The guilt is getting to me."

"Don't you dare do a thing, not a single thing until we tangle through this mess. I will figure it out and then we'll decide what to do. Give me some time."

Time was not on her side. Nick's ghost was hot on her tail, ready to punish her like no jury could.

"I have to turn myself in. It's what he wants. Nick wants justice and he's going to kill me if he doesn't get it."

"You don't know that you did it." But Miriam's fading words betrayed her. A fresh tear trailed down her cheek, resting on her chin.

"I'm screwed. Either way I'm screwed, but at least I can do the right thing."

"I need to find those videos and I will. Please. Give me two days. Keep him at bay for two days. That's all I ask."

"You've got two days. But Miriam?"

"What is it?"

"You've got your answers. I made a mistake—a huge mistake. I let my emotions for Maggie and Ryan take hold

245

of me until I went insane with rage. In my heart I know it's true. Now it's time for you to let go." Her heart ached for Miriam, for the inevitable pain she had caused.

"Two days." Miriam repeated as she grabbed Naomi and held on tightly.

All Naomi could do was mourn for the loss of her and Bryce. There would be no wedding. She was a criminal. Holly wouldn't get her mother figure, after all. There were no winners here, only losers. This entire time she had been playing cat and mouse with Nick, he knew. He would mock her until the bitter end, and the worst part? She deserved it.

CHAPTER THIRTY-ONE

Bryce

KNOCKING ON HER door, Bryce called out over and over for Naomi. She was in there; he knew it because her car sat in the driveway, but why was she closing him out? After numerous attempts at calling and texting, he pounded on her door.

"Naomi! Open the door or I'm breaking it down!"

The possibility that she could be lying there, hurt or worse, sickened him. Come on, Naomi. Come *on*.

"I can't do this right now." Naomi ran a hand through her disheveled head of hair. Dark shadows set off a dull sadness in her eyes.

"Are you okay?" He took hold of her fragile wrists as she stood on the doorstep, grabbing her until she was inches from him. Was she sick?

"I can't—" Naomi pulled away and then waved a dismissive hand at him. She turned to go back inside.

Oh, hell no. Pushing the door forward, he followed her past the entrance foyer and into the kitchen. He could do nothing but watch as she plopped herself in a chair at the kitchen table and slumped her shoulders. Finally, she glanced at him for the briefest of moments before turning her tear-stained face away from him.

"Talk to me. Did I do something?" Bryce couldn't imagine what could evoke such a reaction from her.

"Nope. It was all me. I made a huge freaking mess out of my life and your life all by myself." The inappropriateness of the laughter that followed her statement hitched his breathing.

"Slow down, you're not well. I have no idea what you're talking about."

"You're right about that. I'm not well." The laughter returned. "Funny thing is, I even had myself fooled. Imagine that." Shaking her head, she faced away from him once more.

"Fooled? What happened? Did you change your mind about me? About us?" His stomach dropped as his heart pounded simultaneously. He couldn't lose her. Not now.

"This is bigger than us, Bryce, so much bigger. But no, we can't be together anymore. I'm no good, not for you and not for Holly. I'm sorry—"

Standing there, he attempted to move but his heavy legs would not allow it. "I don't understand."

But slowly, he began to fit the pieces of the puzzle together. This is what she had been getting at before, when he had spoken with her on the phone. The idea of Naomi murdering anyone, even Nick, was impossible. He refused to accept the words that flowed directly from her lips.

"No. Naomi, no." He placed his hands over his ears, blocking out her words.

Her shaking form slowly turned to face him again, tears coursed down her beautiful face. "Yes, Bryce. Yes."

This time, his feet left the floor and he had her crushed in his arms, so tightly that he couldn't imagine anyone would ever be strong enough to tear her away from him. He wouldn't let her go. Nobody could take his girl from him, no one held that power.

Except her.

"Leave please." Her words cut him deeper than a knife as she untangled herself from his embrace.

"No. I'm not leaving you."

A coldness crossed her eyes, "Leave. I don't want you here anymore. Go!"

"You didn't do it, Naomi. You're not the one. I know it, as sure as I know my own name. I'm coming back for you."

She lifted her head to gaze at him. Was it hope or hopelessness he witnessed in her eyes?

HOW MANY TIMES had he been tempted to march right back to Naomi's house? Too many to count. He would not give up or let go. Not now. Not ever.

Naomi's soul and his were entwined together, through all the goodness and the bad. Since he had laid eyes on her, he couldn't imagine living life without her. Hell, even if her suspicions were correct, he would stay by her side. He loved her that much.

Just as Ryan and Maggie's love had crossed the boundaries of time and space, he knew Naomi had touched *his* soul in a way that was both beautiful and unearthly. Their love would break barriers through eternity and he would fight to make Naomi see not only the good in their relationship, but the purity of her own gentle soul.

"Daddy?"

She caught him off guard. Wiping his eyes to clear the tears, he sniffed and faced his daughter.

"Where's Nomi? I want to watch a movie with her. She loves mermaids and her favorite movie of all is on. She told me." Holly's wide eyes met his.

"Oh, honey. She's working, but soon, real soon, she'll watch that movie with you."

Holly narrowed her eyes at Bryce, her little face scrunching in distaste. "Promise?"

Promise? Was he in any position to assure such a thing to his daughter? Holly had been crushed by the absence of her mother and now Naomi's presence in their lives was being challenged.

"She will watch that movie with you, sweetheart."

"Promise?"

"I promise."

Once he made a commitment to anyone, especially his daughter, he kept it. This time, he could only pray he had the power to keep his word.

She needed time and space.

He needed her.

Back at the inn by the beach, he had also made a very crucial vow to stand by Naomi's side and never leave her alone. A man of his word, he lifted his head and swore.

Picking up his cell, he called his sister and asked if he could drop Holly by for a visit.

"Damn, Naomi. You might hate me for this, but I'm coming for you."

CHAPTER THIRTY-TWO

Naomi

INCESSANT BANGING MADE it impossible to fall into the dark, tempting hole of slumber. Damn, it had to be Bryce again. She would give him credit for persistence, but it wasn't enough to make her get up and answer the door. Hating to be cruel, her heart crumbled. Turning her soul mate away had been the hardest thing she had ever done. More difficult than fighting both Nick and Genna together. How could she allow Bryce to get his hopes up when she was destined to live out the rest of her life behind bars? What was the saying? If you love someone set them free? It devastated Naomi to end things, but her very last gift to him must be freedom.

Go away. Go away. "Go away!" Naomi shouted, holding her head. Her hectic thoughts slammed at her, not allowing her any peace. Not one damn minute of peace.

She had some nerve blaming the doctor; although caught having his trysts, he was far from a murderer. And Phil? My God, the man must surely hate her now. She wondered if Miriam had shared Naomi's wild notion that he was the murderer.

"I'm sorry, Ryan. I'm sorry for accusing your brother. I know you two had grown apart, but I also know your heart. He was your big brother and you loved him." Flinching, she thought she felt someone touch her. Nothing. Zelda must have sensed Naomi's troubles as she scooted by her side and pressed her body closer, purring.

Still, the knocking. "Stop it, Bryce! Leave me alone!" But the pounding wasn't coming from the door, it was much closer. Glancing up from her spot on the floor, Naomi sat up straight and peered through the large glass window.

Phil. What could he possibly want right now? A grinning Phil held up her jacket. The one she had forgotten to pick up at Miriam's place.

Really? Now?

He wasn't going away, that much was evident. Fine. Stumbling onto her feet, Naomi ambled her way to the front door. Still holding up the jacket, she forced a saccharin smile and grabbed it from him.

"Thanks, Phil."

"No problem. Miriam was going to pop by with it because she said you would never remember to stop over, but then she got a call to go into work. So I figured I'd save her the trip."

"I appreciate it—"

"Oh, it was nothing. Say, you wouldn't happen to have a cup of coffee, would you?" Poking his head to peer into the entrance foyer, Phil smiled at her. It struck her for the millionth time how much he resembled his brother.

"I'm not really feeling well. Perhaps another time."

"Oh, come on. I'm practically falling asleep at the wheel. Just one cup, promise."

One cup. That shouldn't take long. Maybe it would even edge some of the guilt of accusing him away. Anyway, it would be a distraction from her venomous thoughts.

"One cup. Come on in."

Phil followed Naomi into the kitchen. Just as he walked in the room, Zelda cried an earsplitting howl before sprinting away. Recalling how much Zelda had adored Ryan, she had to say she was stumped. Then again, she had come to learn that while Ryan and Phil might appear similar, they were vastly different in personality.

Brewing the coffee, Naomi attempted small talk, which was proving to be a cumbersome task at best.

"You seem tired, Naomi."

"Yeah, well." She cast her eyes down.

"Yes, I suppose all that investigating can become quite tiresome."

She eyed him warily. Was he being sarcastic or genuine? It was difficult to tell at this point.

"Hard to believe Ryan is gone."

The random comment caught her by surprise. They had never discussed Ryan's death, not since the services last year. "Yes." In her opinion, she wanted to end the conversation there. Enough heartache and sadness loomed over her right now.

"Did Ryan ever tell you the story of how I saved his life?"

His comment brought her back to focus. "No, he didn't say anything about it at all."

"Hm. That surprises me, really. I mean, as close as the two of you were, I figured he'd share something that personal with you."

"No, but continue." Naomi wasn't sure she liked his tone, but was curious to hear about this crucial bit of Ryan's history.

"He always had a bit of a wild side, my little brother. I took pride in looking out for him, like any good older brother would."

Nodding her head, Naomi urged him to continue. The coffee served to refresh her mind and she had to admit it felt better to be alert.

"It was at a New Years' Eve party. Go figure, right?" Phil laughed aloud, although Naomi failed to see the humor. "Ryan was eighteen at the time, and although I wasn't technically invited to the party, I figured I'd stop by just to make sure everything was on the up and up, you know?"

Sipping at her hot coffee, she braced herself for the pivotal part of this story while she watched Phil's eye twitch.

"The one person I didn't expect to see there was my little sister." Waiting out her reaction, he paused.

She nearly choked on her coffee. "Wait—little sister?"

"Yup. She was Ryan's twin." Another pause as the words brought goose bumps.

"I don't— I didn't know he had a twin." It was all she could muster. Why wouldn't Ryan tell her that? Unless…unless it was a memory so harrowing and deep, too painful to expose.

"What happened to her?" Naomi moved forward, on the edge of her seat, the edges of the room fading out behind Phil's face.

"There was a fight. Raegan was a beauty, as I suppose you could imagine Ryan's twin would be. She had this boyfriend, I didn't like him from the start. He was an older man, for starters, about ten years her senior. His jealousy started to show in different ways, but Raegan was such a trusting soul. She thought he just cared for her so much that she didn't see him for what he was."

Naomi recalled when she had first started dating Nick, in the beginning and then when his jealousy took over. Poor thing. "Please, go on."

"An argument between her boyfriend and some stupid, eager guy who had been flirting with Raegan ensued. Once I saw the punches fly, I knew I had been right to come to the party." Phil's eye twitched once more and he looked away for a brief second. When he gazed at Naomi, she could see anger melding with sorrow. Placing her hand on his wrist, she was hurt when he pulled away from her.

"I was too late. I saw her there, in the middle of the struggle. One of the punches landed her on the floor. She died instantly, they say, when her head smashed onto the coffee table."

"What—I—"

"There's nothing to say, Naomi. Not now, not then. If I had been there seconds earlier, I could have prevented the murder."

"Murder?" It had sounded like an awful, horrible accident to her. Chills swept through her as she realized that Ryan had suffered from having had two women he loved taken from him by senseless accidents.

"I'm not finished. Her boyfriend was a cop, he should have known better than to start a fight in the middle of a room full of people drinking, partying. I blamed him, and so did Ryan. I'm not sure if you realize the bond that is shared between twins. Twins can feel the other sibling's emotions, their joy, their pain and their sadness. Raegan's boyfriend fled the scene faster than the speed of light, so that left the other man."

So much sadness and agony. Why hadn't Ryan told her?

"Ryan had just heard Raegan's heart beat for the last time. There was no other option. In a blind rage, my little brother caught up with the man who had so carelessly flirted with Raegan. He chased him to the door, and it was in the driveway that Ryan finally caught him. Looking on, I was helpless to stop. When the other man pulled a small knife from his pocket, Ryan's face had registered shock as he struggled to protect himself. It wasn't his fault—I swear, I was right there, but in the struggle of trying to remove the knife from the other man's hands, Ryan inadvertently stabbed him in the stomach."

"Oh my God. Phil—" Speechless, Naomi cried out, clutching at her chest. She didn't think she could handle much more of this horror that surrounded her like a magnet.

"Don't. Don't embarrass yourself by trying to say something to make this better. It's not going to get better, Naomi. It sucks and there's nothing you or anyone else can say to change the fact that my little sister never got to grow up, that my little brother suffered endless days of torture until some little ass took his life."

She flinched at his harshness, but allowed him to work out his agonizing emotions.

Pondering her words, she had so many questions to ask. "But—it was all a horrible accident. Didn't the police understand?"

"Hell, I wasn't about to take any chances and find out. Turns out the police weren't very understanding after all. I took the rap for the crime and I did the time."

"But why?"

"Why? Because that's what big brothers do. They protect their loved ones. Living out his life without Raegan was enough of a living hell for Ryan. It was my duty, my responsibility, to let Ryan have the opportunity to live his life, to fall in love, raise a family." Phil's voice faded and he seemed to zone out for a moment.

He had fallen in love, but sadly, he and Maggie had never had the chance to start a family. Wiping a tear from her eye, she tried once more to reach out for Phil.

"Don't." He pulled back as if her touch was fire. "Don't make this more difficult than it needs to be."

"What?" Truly, she didn't understand his harsh attitude toward her. Sure, they hadn't gotten off on the best of terms, but his behavior went beyond that.

"You think I don't know that you accused me? You think Miriam would keep that from me? You gotta love it, *you* murder old Nick there and blame me? That's priceless." His deep laughter hit her core as she attempted to back up in her chair. Now Phil's hand smashed down, pinning her arm to the table.

"You're hurting me. Let me go." Naomi wouldn't whimper—she projected her voice firmly. *Don't let him see your fear.* "I admit I was wrong and I cleared it up with Miriam. You're right, I am the murderer and I'll do what's right. I'm prepared to confess."

259

An odd look came over Phil, as he tightened his grip on her. "You are crazy, you know that? Don't mock me. You know as well as I did you didn't do it, so stop messing with me. I know if I let you go you would rat me out in a second. I have to give you credit. You did it— you solved the murder. Are you proud of yourself?"

Fear was not her first emotion upon hearing his words. Elation and relief danced in front of her, so close she could almost grab them.

Almost. If not for the dangerous man facing her. She wasn't losing her mind, she was not the murderer. She *was not* the killer. Naomi would marry Bryce, have a life with her new family. She released the cold, hard breath she had been holding for so long and surprised both Phil and herself by forcing her way up, out of his grasp.

She should have just made a run for it, but she wouldn't have gotten too far, she realized as Phil produced a sleek black pistol. She knew it was one of Miriam's guns she kept at home in the safe because Miriam had shown her how to shoot a gun at the shooting range using that exact weapon.

"Your prints are already all over it, I don't even have to worry about that. You went mad and shot yourself. Couldn't take the pain and guilt that comes with being a murderer." Phil chuckled harshly before continuing. "Oh, and I thought I did a pretty good job forging your signature on the logs by the way. It only took sneaking in here and grabbing a copy from your filing cabinet to do it."

"No." It was a mere whisper as she backed toward the entranceway. No wonder the papers on her desk had been a mess that day. She had wrongly blamed Zelda. Phil had obviously transferred her signature over his own on all of the papers at the jail.

"Yup. I'm afraid it's the only way. You see, I can't have Miriam connecting the dots. Oh, and by the way, I lied. I was eavesdropping on Miriam's conversation with you. She would never share your suspicions with me. She was ridiculous when it came to defending anything you did."

"It's called friendship, Phil, something you've obviously never discovered."

"You know, you're not really in a position to be taunting me. If I were you I would keep that mouth of yours shut and listen. I'm not finished—when I tell a story, I tell it to the end."

Gulping, Naomi silently prayed for Maggie to work her charms. Where was that deliciously eerie screech Maggie had dredged up in times of trouble? One thing that brought relief was knowing that Bryce would stay away because of how cold she had been toward him.

Come on, Maggie. Come on.

"As I was saying, Raegan's boyfriend is the one who holds the most blame in this story of mine. If it weren't for his twisted jealousy, my sister would be alive today."

Nonsense spewed from Phil's lips as Naomi mentally calculated her escape plan. Problem was, options were slim with a gun pointed squarely at her.

"Phil—"

"Shut up and listen! You have a rude habit of interrupting, do you know that? Raegan's boyfriend needed to be punished. I bided my time in prison and when I was finally released, I made a point of returning to finish my business. I thought to myself, what's the best way to hurt someone? Sure, I could have killed the boyfriend himself, but what better way to exact revenge than have the punishment fit the crime?"

"I don't know what you're talking about." Naomi noticed the fact that Phil kept referring to the man who had been Raegan's boyfriend as merely "the boyfriend."

"Who was he? What was the name of Raegan's boyfriend?"

Ignoring her question, Phil continued to rant. "Little did I know that by the time I had returned, the plot had continued."

No wonder Ryan had claimed his brother lived far away; that way he didn't have to share that the reason he and Phil had lost touch was because Phil had been serving time. This also explained why Ryan had taken off, exploring the country for years before returning to this area. He had grown up several towns away, she had learned.

"All along, I had planned to kill his nephew—the only relative he seemed to care about. Little did I know at the time that I had another very good reason to kill the man."

"Wait—his nephew?" Flashes of faces came to mind: Nick, Uncle Frank. Uncle Frank? A sick sinking feeling nearly stole her breath. Too much information flitted around in her mind; she couldn't comprehend where one thought began and one ended.

Although she had always thought of Nick's uncle as being much older, now that she actually thought about it, she realized he wasn't. It was something about his strict ways and harsh temperament that made him seem older.

"It was Uncle Frank?" she sputtered, forcing her eyes open.

"Bingo." Pointing the pistol closer, she squeezed her eyes tight, wishing again for Maggie to appear. It hit her now why Ryan had remained absent throughout this entire mess. He must have been torn, caught between protecting the big brother who had saved him from years in prison—or as Phil had put it, saved his life—and helping Naomi put Nick to rest by solving the murder. Now she understood what Maggie had been trying to tell her– that Ryan had been the one blocking her.

Oh, Ryan.

"Say good night, Naomi." Pinned by the wall behind her and the gun in front of her, she had nowhere to turn, but she would be damned if she was going down without a fight. Kicking him below the belt with all the strength she could muster, Naomi then lunged for the door. Screaming out obscenities, Phil tackled her, overpowering her with his sheer strength. "Bad move, Naomi. Now you've gone and pissed me off," he spat in her face.

She closed her eyes as his finger pressed down slowly on the trigger. *I'm sorry, Bryce. I love you.*

"Don't do it, Phil."

Sobbing openly at the familiar voice, she cried out for her friend. "Ryan!" There he stood as she drank in every amazing inch of that tall, dark, and handsome man. Pinned by Phil, she struggled to breathe.

"What the—" Phil's face turned a pale shade of green. "Ryan?"

"Let her go."

"Ryan? I didn't believe all this crap they told me about ghosts, but it's you, isn't it?" Still, he held on to Naomi as he peered up at Ryan. "I'm sorry. I can't go back to prison, it nearly killed me. I'm sorry, Ryan but you'll understand this all comes back to you and Raegan."

"Raegan and I are together, in peace. Let Naomi go or I'll never forgive you. I'll no longer consider you to be my brother."

"I can't Ryan, I can't."

Using all her will to look up, her eyes pleaded with Ryan, begging him to do more, to help her in any possible way.

"I love that girl and if you kill her, I'll never be the same."

Phil's eyes darted between Naomi and Ryan and for a second; she actually saw part of a wall to start the crumble, but then just as quickly the wall returned. "I'm sorry. Forgive me, Ryan."

Finger on the trigger once more, Naomi could only take solace in Ryan's presence. It would be thoughts of Ryan and love for Bryce that gave her the courage to pass to the other side. Closing her eyes, Naomi prepared for the end.

"Naomi!"

Had she imagined his face? At that moment he appeared, her knight in shining armor, just like in the fairy tales. But this wasn't a tale. This was Naomi's life, which was tragically coming to an end. What better vision to end her life with than the image of Bryce's love?

Heavy weight punched her in the gut as Naomi's body slammed to the side with force. She struggled to make sense of the scene before her. Bryce now wrestled with Phil, the gun glaring steadily in Phil's hands.

"No! Don't hurt him! Leave him alone!" Naomi cried out as she saw Phil's hand squeezing in, gripping the gun tightly. His finger pressed down and the sickening boom of thunder, right there in her very own kitchen, tore her soul to pieces.

No. This couldn't be happening.

Not Bryce.

"Bryce, Bryce, Bryce," she wailed, crawling to him on her hands and knees. He lifted his head, his precious, beautiful head, and stared right at her.

"Come here." He pushed a groaning Phil off of him and handed the gun to Naomi. "Don't let go of that."

"Is he—?"

"From the looks of it, he'll be okay."

Naomi could see the blood gushing from Phil's shoulder as he gasped in pain. She jumped up and reached for her cell phone as Miriam shot through the front door.

"Naomi!"

"I'm okay, I'm okay." She held her arms out for Miriam and the two women clung to one another.

"I was a fool. He had the video destroyed but what he didn't know was that Crackers squealed like a baby. Under pressure and the threat of permanent solitary confinement, he told me everything," Miriam exclaimed. "Please forgive me."

She wouldn't allow her friend to venture down the path of self-doubt and guilt. Heck–everyone was human, everyone made foolish mistakes, especially where matters of the heart were concerned.

Even Miriam Marty.

"Of course, but let's not do this. Not now. Right now, I want to hold my loved ones tightly and never let go." She motioned for Bryce to join them. Reaching out for Naomi and Miriam, Bryce leaned in and whispered in Naomi's ear.

"He loves you. I saw Ryan, standing there beside us during the struggle. He did it, he saved my life for you."

And just then, a vision appeared of Ryan, pushing the gun away from Bryce and in the direction of Phil's shoulder, a split second before it went off.

Then, she had never seen anything as beautiful as she witnessed gazing up at Ryan's retreating form. She saw the words form on his lips moments before he disappeared.

She repeated them aloud to him in return. "I love you, too, my friend," she whispered.

It was then that Naomi could feel the love he must have felt for Raegan and why it had been too painful to speak of his sister. Naomi and Ryan's relationship had been one that had started as two people dating, just getting to know one another. What had transpired between the two was a bond far greater than they could have shared as lovers. She had always felt more like a sister than a girlfriend to him, and now she knew: his heart had been searching for love– pure love, like that he had given to his sister. In the end, he had given another piece of his heart to her and that was a gift that couldn't be taken from her, in life and in death.

Smiling down at her, she saw Maggie standing arm in arm beside the stunning young woman with jet-black hair and the same sparkling blue eyes of the man she had grown to love with all of her heart—not in the same way as Bryce, but in her heart she had more than enough room for both men.

A wave of peacefulness fell over her, watching Maggie and Raegan standing together. The world seemed to make sense again.

"You okay?" Bryce ran a hand through her mop of hair.

"I am, Bryce. I finally am."

CHAPTER THIRTY-THREE

Naomi

NOW THAT SHE had her answers concerning the mystery of Nick's murder, she figured logically that the final step would be to confront Nick and say a long overdue farewell to his spirit and the negativity that surrounded it.

Between the three of them—Naomi, Bryce, and Miriam—they had put together all of the missing pieces to their conundrum. It was easy to see how Phil's connection with Johnny Clarke had come to pass. While on the inside himself, Phil had made connections and reaches to this area. Once he had found that Nick would be difficult to harm in prison, he called on his favors from inmates he had formed relationships with.

The visits to the prison to speak with Crackers had been easy enough to secure and helping to make the log disappear had been a joint effort between Crackers and a crooked prison guard.

The most challenging part of the scheme, they had learned from a belligerent Crackers, had been the actual overdose. That was, in fact, a joint effort between Phil and Crackers. Phil had coerced Crackers to find someone to slip into the medication area and substitute the five milligram dose pills with the forty milligram dose. Although the pills differed in size and color, Nick didn't question the illegal supply he had arranged to receive on a regular basis. In addition to the small white pills he received from the prison doctor for pain, the yellow ones were what did him in.

Apparently during Nick's time in jail, his addiction had increased ten-fold and he had plenty of shady friends to help feed his growing need. So, bottom line, Phil had not worked alone. Crackers was, well Crackers, so his part in exposing both Phil and himself so easily surprised no one that knew him well. Heck, he may have been high on something himself when he sang like a canary.

Four days had passed without a sign from Nick. Naomi had started to wonder if Nick already knew justice had been served and therefore had left her house, going to places unknown.

But she was smart enough not to let her guard down. Not yet. Which explained why she didn't so much as flinch when she heard the noise come from the other side of her office.

As usual, Zelda hightailed it out of the room as Naomi sat up straighter, unafraid now of what was to come.

Out of the shadows of the far closet he came, expressionless in the increasingly frigid room. Sitting taller still, Naomi's eyes opened wide, showing him no fear.

What he did next should have surprised her, but it didn't, because once upon a time, quite a while ago, this man had been fond of her. Had he ever loved her? Nick didn't know the meaning of the word love, but fondness? Yeah, she supposed Nick could do fondness.

She stood up, now face-to-face with this demon, and held her ground. "I'm through, Nick. You got what you wanted, now leave me be."

Wild wind from the cold night air entered the room as her windowpane shattered with the force of his sorrow. *I will not let him scare me. I will not let him see my weakness.*

He touched her then, and she sucked in a burning breath. He filled her with the sadness of a little boy who grew up raised by a neglectful aunt and uncle who showed their distaste for Nick and the task of raising a child they had never prepared for. Eventually, as a young adult, she saw Uncle Frank's feelings for Nick grow and she could see that although Frank had many issues, he would protect his nephew, and even care for him.

In her soul, she felt the anguish and the rejection. In school, the other kids ridiculed him for his unkempt appearance and tough attitude, which had been apparent even when he was so young.

It hurt beyond anything Naomi could have imagined and he had placed it all inside of her mind. "Don't. Please don't do this, Nick. You can be better than this."

Nick's voice broke, letting Naomi see his vulnerability for probably the first time since she had known him. "I see this love you have for everyone. I've watched you with Bryce, Miriam, Maggie, Ryan, and Holly. How can you have that much love and never have shown it to me?"

He wanted love?

That's what he had been after this entire time? Standing before her now, Nick blew her mind with his admission.

"You solved the crime, Naomi. I knew you could and I knew you would. But what I wanted more than anything was a piece of your heart."

Nick wanted someone to love him unconditionally, the way a parent does. The way he had never been loved. "Why, Nick? Why were you always so angry and bitter? You hurt me, you could have *killed* me."

Shaking his head, he reached out and touched her cheek ever so delicately. "I'm an angry soul. At first I didn't even know what I wanted from you myself. All I felt, all I saw was rage and frustration at what had become of my life. It consumed me. But the more I watched you, the more I really got to know you as a person like I never had the time to in the past. I wanted what you gave so freely and openly to those people lucky enough to be called your friends."

"Oh, Nick." It would be so difficult to forgive him after everything he had done, both to herself and to Maggie and Ryan. But it had been a horrifying accident with Maggie and Ryan and she recalled Maggie's wish for her to let go of her anger and forgive.

If ever there was a role model to look up to, it was Maggie. Gazing at his tear-stained face, she held his hand and closed her eyes tightly.

"I'm afraid to go on, in the afterlife with this much bitterness. What will become of me?"

Trying to concentrate, she attempted to tune him out as she felt a small transformation taking place in her own heart for the man standing before her.

"I'm scared, Naomi. So scared." His eyes pleaded with her. "Help me."

Quiet. Be quiet.

Her focused emotions took hold of her and this time, when she attempted to forgive him for all the bad he had done, her heart opened wider, just enough to fit a piece of him within her forever.

Opening her eyes, she gazed at him and saw a slight difference in the set of his jaw, the lines of his face, and finally the dark shadows under his eyes, which had all but vanished, leaving his eyes bright and clear.

"Nick." Gone was the wild, reckless, and jealous man she had come to know and fear. His softened features told her everything she needed to know. Reaching for both of her hands, he held them firmly.

"I knew you had enough love in that heart of yours to give me just one tiny piece. It's all I've ever wanted—from anyone. I've been searching for this my entire life." Lifting her chin gently, he leaned in and kissed her lips so lightly, so delicately, for the quickest of moments, that she could scarcely feel his touch.

"Thank you. It's all I ever wanted." He repeated the phrase once more as he released her and his form faded. She stood, alone, clutching at her heart, basking in the warmth of realization. This man had just learned about the meaning of love for the first time and her gut told her it wasn't too late for him.

Tenderness touched her from deep within, as a small smile began to play on her lips. She realized then that Nick's story might have a place not just in her heart, but in one of her future novels as well.

EPILOGUE

Naomi

Standing before her was the man Naomi's soul had always yearned for. Bryce moved a strand of sea-swept hair from before her eyes. Naomi's heart melted just a tiny bit more as she swallowed back the aching in her throat. Bryce had the power to bring her to tears, but this time the tears came not from frustration or fear, but from the pure adoration she felt as she had listened to his emotional pledge. She had practiced her own vows over and over the past few days and now it was her turn.

Glancing around, she took in the fading light of the beach, wishing to imprint this memory in her mind. Her loved ones smiled at her, their eyes urging her on, giving her their unspoken support. Miriam sat pin-straight, Mr. and Mrs. Field on one side while Amy, Kristen and Jackson sat on the other.

If only things could have turned out differently for Miriam. Naomi knew Miriam didn't trust easily, and that Phil's betrayal would sting for a while. But Naomi also knew it wouldn't sting for too long, because Miriam was a rock and would come out even stronger as a result of her experience.

Maggie's mother wiped a tear from her eye and Naomi could only imagine the emotions that had to be gripping hold of her. Mr. Field placed his hand on his wife's thigh as Naomi felt her heart pull for the couple.

Soon, the sun would go down and she would become Bryce's wife. Each and every person in attendance had a piece of her heart, including the little girl tugging on her arm.

"Nomi!" Holly's exclamation startled her, bringing her back to the present.

"I'm waiting, beautiful," Bryce whispered, taking hold of her hands as his eager eyes locked with hers.

With the slightest tremble in her voice, she spoke, softly at first, wondering how she could make it through without breaking down in tears. *Like an emotional basket case*, she thought to herself with a small grin.

"Bryce, no one else in this world could have made this journey with me. I mean, who else would put up with the circus that has surrounded me since we met?" Laughter erupted and it gave her the push to continue, her tone more confident now.

"Not only did you stand by my side, but you joined me there, in a place that I couldn't have survived without knowing you were there to catch me in the end." Naomi felt a warm tear slide down her cheek, matching Bryce's own tears.

"And Holly." Holly's eyes sparkled at the sound of her name being spoken aloud. "I'm honored to call you my family. I cherish you as I cherish your father. You make me smile each and every day, sweetheart." Holly grinned widely as Naomi bent down to kiss her on her tiny cheek.

Next, she clutched Holly's hand with one hand and then reached for Bryce's hand with the other. This strength she felt when the three of them were together was what made life worth living, These were her people and she would hold them tightly, never letting go, not for one moment.

"I love you more than I can express." Naomi breathed in deeply, her heart thumping loudly in her chest. "Bryce, Holly?" She gazed expectantly from one face to the other. "I'm ready. I'm ready to do this."

Bryce pulled her in close, placing his hands on either side of her face. "Honey, we're already there." His warm lips caressed hers, pressing down, sealing their fate.

Bryce

At times, the pain and hurt came back, but only momentarily. One look at Naomi's beautiful face and the heartache all but disappeared. It had been worse, so much harder for her, of course. But here she was, all his, smiling brightly in the fading light, easing away all of the stress and tension from the past few months.

When he had learned of Nick's ultimate purpose, part of him had been taken aback that Naomi ultimately gave in to his request: part of her heart for a miscreant such as Nick. But then Bryce considered that the very thing that attracted him to Naomi *was* her huge heart and she certainly proved she had more than enough of her love to share.

He supposed what bothered him most was the big question: Did Nick really deserve it? But that was Naomi; she tended to see the good in people, even people such as Nick. He didn't consider her naïve, not in the least. She had been through hell and back with Nick and still saw the hopeless little boy who had been searching for someone to love and accept him.

From that moment when Bryce had proposed and carved their initials right beside those belonging to Maggie and Ryan on that tree by the cliff, he had known she was one in a million.

Days ago, they had traveled back to Jane's Ending for their wedding ceremony. Now, under a starlit sky, he sat by the fire on the beach, slowly turning a marshmallow for an exuberant Holly.

Holly would have her wish granted after all; she would watch that mermaid movie with Naomi. If he broke that promise to his daughter, his heart wouldn't have survived.

His wife laughed aloud at something Kristen and Jackson were saying, but attuned to each other as usual, she took that exact moment to stop and peer back at him. Her glance bounced between him and Holly as she whispered the words he would always cherish. He could never get enough of her and it hit him at that precise moment that of all the people in the world Nick's soul could have hoped to have been touched by, it was his wife.

It was Naomi—and he knew why.

THE END

ACKNOWLEDGEMENTS

I always worry that I'm going to leave someone out when it's time to sit and write my acknowledgements. As usual, I received an overwhelming amount of love from many, many people in my life, for which I am extremely grateful.

Alexandra, thank you for sharing your love of all things paranormal. You continue to inspire me to share these mysterious stories involving ghosts and the unknown. I'm waiting for you to write your own novel one day soon. I just know it will be amazing.

Mom, thank you for your support with this novel as well as with all of my others books as well. I appreciate all of the time you dedicate to discussing my stories and sharing your feedback.

Mom, Dad, Jimmer, Damian, Amanda, and Siobhan–thank you for being there for me and supporting all that I do. Siobhan– once again, thanks for letting me come by your house to wander around and get inspiration for the setting of *Naomi* as I did for *Maggie*. From your home to your property, it's the perfect location for my characters to come to life. Sorry of that's just a little bit creepy! (laughs)

Thank you, Alan, for listening to many variations of my plot and helping me to bounce ideas around. I appreciate your feedback and support.

I wanted to acknowledge my oldest friends for being there for me, for just listening and sharing your friendship. Kim, Janine, Karen, Jim, and Jen–thank you.

My street team is made up of some pretty amazing people. I'm so thankful for each and every one of you for all that you do—from beta reading to helping me promote, to just chatting and having a nice time getting to know one another.

Dawn Yacovetta, thank you again for all of your help and valuable feedback. I appreciate everything you do.

Jena Brignola, thanks for another amazing cover. You have made each of my visions for my covers become a reality for me.

I can't express how thankful I am to Sara Meadows, my editor for Naomi. Thank you for everything, including being a wonderful PA and friend. (I think I was much calmer self -publishing this time around!)

Lastly, I would like to thank my readers for your ongoing support. I love hearing the feedback I get from each of you and love nothing more than sharing my stories with you.

The characters in both *Maggie* and *Naomi* hold such a special place in my heart. Thank you to everyone for letting me share them with you.

You can follow me at:
www.myaomalley.com,
Instagram @myaomalley
Facebook.com/myaomalley

XOXO
Mya